she continued, "If you don't leave me alone, I shall scream."

"Let me buy you this perfume," he cut in.

"No!" she snapped, rage in her green eyes. "I loathe it! It will always remind me of you!"

"In that case," he drawled, "I shall buy you a very large bottle of it. You must keep it in your bedroom. Then you'll always think of me as you undress."

SARAH HOLLAND was born in Kent and brought up in London. She began writing at eighteen because she loved the warmth and excitement of romance novels. She has traveled the world—living in Hong Kong, the South of France and Holland. She attended drama school, and was a nightclub singer and a songwriter. She now lives on the Isle of Man. Her hobbies are acting, singing, painting and psychology. She loves buying clothes, noisy dinner parties and being busy.

SARAH HOLLAND

Extreme Provocation

Harlequin Books

TORONTO • NEW YORK • LONDON
AMSTERDAM • PARIS • SYDNEY • HAMBURG
STOCKHOLM • ATHENS • TOKYO • MILAN
MADRID • WARSAW • BUDAPEST • AUCKLAND

ISBN 0-373-18604-5

EXTREME PROVOCATION

First North American Publication 1995.

This edition published by arrangement with Harlequin Enterprises B.V.

Printed in U.S.A.

CHAPTER ONE

LUCY stepped out of the taxi into the warm night air. Looking up at Marlborough's, the exclusive London casino, she shivered, drawing her white lace shawl closer around her bare shoulders.

There was nothing else for it. She had to go into this imposing place and get her father. He had already spent most of her grandfather's fortune since inheriting it. If Lucy couldn't stop him, he would gamble himself into bankruptcy and ruin.

Marlborough's was a private gambling club for the very rich. A doorman in smart livery demanded her name and proof of her identity.

'Lucy Winslow,' she said haughtily, handing him her passport. 'My father is Gerald Winslow.'

He tilted his cap and motioned for the doors to be opened.

She swept in, head held high. Luxury surrounded her in the cream-gold foyer with its high ceiling and crystal chandeliers. Gazing around, she felt suddenly very young and naïve, not sure where to go. Where were the gaming rooms? What did one do?

Suddenly she sensed someone watching her. With a start, she looked up, green eyes huge.

A man stood on the luxurious stairs, one hand on a gold banister. He was very tall with broad shoulders and long legs. He wore a black suit, impeccably cut, a dark red silk tie and a tight black waistcoat.

'Feeling lost?' he asked, and his voice was excitingly smoky.

Her pulses leapt. 'No. I was looking for someone.'

The man walked coolly down the stairs. 'Anyone in particular?'

'My father,' she said, staring at his face as he stepped into the light, seeing the jagged scar on his hard-boned cheek, the cynical blue eyes and the firm, ruthless mouth.

'What's his name?' A frown drew black brows together.

'Gerald Winslow,' she said, lifting her blonde head with pride.

'I know him,' he said slowly. 'Come with me.' He opened the door with one very powerful hand. She noticed dark hairs on the back of that hand, white cuffs at his wrist, and the glimpse of a black Rolex watch.

Stepping into the casino, Lucy was dazzled by the expensive gleam of low-lighting on roulette tables, blackjack tables, pontoon and punto banco and the glitter of silver chips, gold chips, scarlet chips, all clattering down polished chutes.

The door swung shut as the dark stranger stepped in beside her. 'This way...' His strong hand moved to the small of her back, propelling her across the luxurious, imposing gaming rooms.

Heads lifted as they passed. Women eyed the stranger admiringly, one sultry brunette even licking her red lips as she watched him stride with cool arrogance past her, his face expressionless.

He led her to a set of doors and opened one. Lucy looked into the baccarat room and saw her father. 'Oh! There he is!' She moved forwards.

'You can't go in.' The man blocked her path.

Lucy's green eyes sparkled up at him. 'But I can see him. He's the one in the——'

'I know which one he is,' he drawled coolly, 'but I'm not letting you in. Not in that dress.' The blue eyes moved to her body with ruthless sexual appraisal, stripping her of the cream silk evening gown that skimmed her full breasts and tiny waist and rounded hips. 'You'd cause a riot,' he murmured insolently.

Hot colour flooded her face. 'You're impertinent,' she said tautly. 'Mr...?'

He smiled slowly and did not reply.

Lucy's mouth tightened. 'I came here to see my father, and I must insist you let me through.'

'You can see him when he's finished playing.' He closed the door and took her bare arm in a cool hand, propelling her away from the room.

Lucy tried to pull away from him. 'What do you think you're doing? Let me go at once!'

'I'll leave word with the floor manager,' he drawled coolly, continuing to stride across the luxurious casino with her. 'He'll send your father to me when the game is over.' He looked down with narrowed eyes, adding, 'Don't cause a scene.'

'I'm not,' she said tensely. 'But I don't know you and I don't like the way you're ordering me around.'

'No need for alarm,' he said flatly. 'You're perfectly safe.'

She gave an angry laugh. 'If I'm perfectly safe, why are you trying to take me somewhere?'

'Because I can see you're not used to casino life,' he said coolly, and halted, looking down at her with those unnerving blue eyes. 'I thought you'd prefer a cup of coffee in a quiet room.'

Hesitating, her eyes darted over his tough face. 'What sort of quiet room?'

'My office,' he said.

Lucy studied him for a moment, the idea appealing to her. She felt out of her depth in this sophisticated atmosphere. However exclusive, there was an edge to the scent of money that was excitingly sinful.

'You work here?' she asked at length.

A smile touched the sardonic mouth. 'Oh, yes...' His long-fingered hand pressured her with the merest touch. 'This way...'

With misgivings, Lucy allowed him to lead her behind the tables. One or two of the men in dark suits who worked behind the tables tried to approach the man. He waved a strong hand of dismissal at them, his face and eyes hard as he strode past with Lucy.

She wondered who he was. He had an air of power and authority. His clothes were impeccably cut. He was obviously very rich. Her eyes scanned his tough face in a sidelong glance. Was he the manager?

'In here,' he said, unlocking a large cream door with a round gold handle and ushering her in.

Lucy moved inside, her pale silvery hair brushing faintly against the man's powerful chest. The door closed with a cool click. Lucy spun, watching him warily through her long fair lashes. Now that she was alone with him in this quiet, civilised room, he seemed even more dangerous.

'Coffee, then?' he asked, strolling coolly towards her.

'Thank you, that would be nice.'

He smiled, and moved to the mahogany desk which, she noticed with surprise, was a French antique. It had exquisite carved legs, the wood rich and deeply polished.

'Two coffees in my office,' he said into the telephone, then punched out another number. 'Send Winslow to me when he's finished playing. Yes . . . my office.' He replaced the receiver. His blue eyes flashed to her face. 'Sit down,' he said softly, gesturing to a long, deep red couch behind her.

Lucy sank down on to it. As she crossed her long slim legs with a swish of silk, his eyes moved assessingly over them. He was unsmiling.

He watched her for a moment, then strolled coolly to the front of the desk and perched on it, his black jacket falling back, exposing the lean power of his body beneath the black waistcoat.

'So you're Gerald Winslow's daughter?'

'Yes.' Lucy watched him through her lashes.

'Are you his only daughter?' His tone was cool, conversational, belying the danger in those ruthless blue eyes as they moved slowly over her, undressing her.

'His only child,' she said, equally conversational, although her pulses were leaping with awareness. 'My mother died when I was four. My father never remarried.'

A frown touched his brow. 'He brought you up alone?'

'Not really.' She laughed lightly. 'There was my grandfather, too.'

'Ah, yes...' The blue eyes narrowed thoughtfully. 'Sir Charles. I remember him. He came here once, with your father. An impressive man. Sharp with cards, too.' He smiled with lazy amusement. 'Made mincemeat of my dealers, if I remember rightly, and walked off with over ten thousand pounds in cash.'

Lucy's green eyes shone with pride and regret. 'He was very clever. We all miss him very much.'

He studied her for a moment, then said, 'And what of you, Miss . . . ?'

'Winslow,' she said, green eyes teasing him through her lashes.

'I wanted your Christian name,' he murmured, a dark look in his eyes.

'Lucy,' she supplied, lifting her chin.

He smiled, said softly, 'Lucy…' and then his blue eyes were moving over her body with sexual appraisal, lingering on her full breasts, bare beneath the revealing cream silk gown. 'It suits you. Especially in that dress. Did you know there were several very famous kings' courtesans called Lucy?'

Hot colour swept slowly up her throat and then her face. She felt suddenly afraid of him, her body pulsing with alarmed excitement.

As if he sensed her fear, he veiled his eyes and smiled. 'And what do you do with yourself all day, Lucy? Are you still at school?'

'No,' she said tensely, lifting her blonde brows haughtily. 'I'm twenty-three, as a matter of fact, and I have a job.'

The hard mouth crooked. 'Do you?'

'Yes.' She felt flustered and under threat. 'I work at a nursery in Kensington. I look after three-year-olds before they go to prep school.'

'And how long have you——?' He broke off as there was a knock at the door. Getting up from the desk, he strode coolly to open it, ushering in a sophisticated brunette in casino evening gown, who placed a tray on the desk, then exited.

When they were alone again, he poured coffee from the silver pot. She watched him through her lashes, aware of the scent of his aftershave as he leant close to her, putting the cups down slowly, then moving back to stand over her, hands sliding into trouser pockets as he watched her with those cynical eyes.

Lucy shifted, unnerved by his gaze.

Suddenly, he sat down beside her, one powerful arm sliding along the couch behind her pale head.

'I wonder if my father's ready yet...' Lucy said, shaken.

'I doubt it,' he murmured, his eyes fixed on her mouth. 'He tends to play till dawn.'

'I can't stay here that long...'

'Don't worry,' he said softly, 'he'll come along when he's ready.' His hand moved slowly, picking up a strand of her blonde hair. 'Is it natural? It's quite the most extraordinary colour.'

'I think I ought to——' she began huskily, trying to get up.

He moved swiftly, surely, his left hand on her bare shoulder as he pushed her gently back against the couch, his dark head looming suddenly over her.

'Not just yet,' he said, watching her through black lashes, and gave a slow, rather deadly smile. 'After all...you don't even know my name.'

She studied him warily, her pulses thudding. 'And what is your name?'

'Randal,' he said, and his strong hand moved slowly to her naked throat.

Panic erupted in her veins. 'Let me go...'

'I'm afraid I can't, my dear,' he said thickly, suddenly very dangerous indeed as his dark head lowered. 'I've wanted to kiss you since I first saw you, and I can assure you you're not leaving this office until I do...'

His dark head seemed to obliterate the light as it lowered, and she felt hypnotised, staring as her heart banged louder and louder until that ruthless mouth closed over hers.

The hot rush of excitement made her gasp, struggling, and that seemed to inflame him.

Suddenly, his mouth was parting hers with hungry demand, and Lucy moaned in hoarse disbelief, her mouth opening helplessly beneath his. But still she struggled, her hands hitting his powerful shoulders, her body wriggling as she tried to push him away.

Her puny fight inflamed him further. A rough sound of pleasure came from the back of his throat. He was pushing her back against the cushions, his mouth a hot onslaught of commanding power, and as his strong hands began to move over her body she gave a hoarse cry of alarmed excitement.

Her hands slapped and scratched at his face and neck. She was fighting in earnest now, a wildcat unleashed in his powerful arms, and then her nails caught his hard jaw with a livid scratch.

'You little cat!' he laughed thickly, jerking his head back from her, but his face was darkly flushed and his blue eyes glittering.

Lucy almost fell off the couch, heart pounding as she grabbed her bag and ran to the door, wrenching it open. He watched her from the couch, his blue eyes narrowed, blood on his hard jaw. He did not attempt to follow her, but there was a hard smile on his mouth, and Lucy was terrified he might.

Running across the casino, she attracted startled looks. She didn't care. Nor did she care that she had left her white shawl in Randal's office. She stumbled out of the casino into the warm night air in time to see a taxi discharging passengers on the steps.

'Astor Square!' she gasped out to the driver as she leapt in and slammed the door. 'Hurry.'

The wheels spun, the taxi pulled away, and as it swung around the corner away from Marlborough's she knew she was safe, though her hands were shaking.

Anger flooded her as she remembered the insolent way he had looked at her, and the ruthless way he had simply taken that kiss from her against her will.

How dared he do that! He had lured her into that office, pretending to be friendly, with the express purpose of kissing her! She could see it all now, from the moment he saw her to the moment he took her into his office, right down to the moment he sank down on the sofa beside her, smiling at her sardonically and looking at her mouth.

Fury sparkled in her green eyes. If she ever saw that man again, she'd slap his hard, handsome face until it stung.

As for her father... a sigh broke from her lips. There was nothing she could do to stop him gambling tonight. He probably wouldn't be home until the early hours of the morning, and how much money would he have lost by then?

Angrily, she thought of Randal preventing her from going into the baccarat room. If he had allowed her entry, she could have been with her father now, in this taxi, driving safely home. The selfishness of the man made her even more furious. No doubt he had more money than he knew what to do with. Certainly, he wouldn't understand Lucy's desperation to save her father from bankruptcy.

The taxi dropped her in Astor Square and she went inside, accustomed to the elegant silence of the house.

Although she lay awake until three, she did not hear her father come home, drunk, at dawn.

Next day, she went to work as usual at the kindergarten in the leafy little residential street in Kensington. The children were in high spirits, and she was covered in paint at the end of the day, and needed to wash her face and arms vigorously.

She walked home in the late-afternoon sunlight. Astor Square was one of the more secluded squares in Kensington, with a pretty little green enclosed by railings, and rows of small detached Georgian houses around it. Her family had once owned the whole of one side of it.

Sir Charles Winslow, her grandfather, had been knighted by the Queen for his contribution to British architecture. Before he died, he had invested all his money in property, buying half of this square to safeguard the money he left to his only son, Gerald.

But since his death, ten years ago, the family fortunes had dwindled to almost nothing. Her father had wanted cash to spend, not investments to retain. House after house had been sold off. Now, they only retained number one, the first house on the square, and Lucy knew her father had taken out a mortgage on it last year.

When she got in, she found her father already drinking.

He was a tall, debonair man in his early fifties with pale blonde hair, silvering at the temples. 'Hello, darling.' he said with lazy charm when he saw her enter the elegant drawing-room. 'Edward and I are just having pre-dinner cocktails. Care to join us?'

Lucy's green eyes flicked with love to Edward's face. 'You shouldn't encourage him.'

Edward gave a wry shrug. 'He'd do it with or without my permission. You know that, Lucy.'

Gerald frowned. 'I say. Don't talk about a chap as though he wasn't here!'

They all laughed.

Edward moved towards Lucy, his pale blue eyes tracing her face with affection. 'You look radiant. Good day with the children?'

'Lovely,' she nodded. 'Come into the kitchen and talk to me while I prepare dinner.'

They went into the kitchen, a bright sunlit room backing on to a small square of garden. Lucy waited until the door was shut, then flung herself into Edward's arms.

'Darling!' She kissed his neck, breathed in the familiar scent of his skin. 'If only you lived here, you could help me stop him. I'm so worried...'

'My darling.' He stroked her hair with long fingers. 'I know. So am I. But I just can't stop him spending. I keep telling him he's hurtling towards bankruptcy, but he won't listen.'

'He's been rich all his life,' she said, closing her eyes. 'He thinks it'll never run out.'

'I've explained it all a thousand times to him.' Edward gave a harsh sigh. 'But it's no good, Lucy. It's as though he wants to destroy himself, and take the family down with him.'

Edward Blair was tall and thin with pale hair and pale skin and a very pale mouth. His father had been Sir Charles's accountant. Edward had naturally taken up the position when his father died. The Winslow family and the Blair family had had a close tie.

Edward was so close to her that he was almost family. She had always known she was in love with him—and that they would one day marry. So had Edward. It was just a matter now of buying a ring and naming the day.

'Edward, I went to the casino last night,' Lucy told him now, 'to try and stop him gambling, but——'

'You went to the casino!' He was shocked. 'My God, Lucy! You shouldn't have done that. Not alone...'

'Why not?' she protested, flushing deeply at the memory of that man's passionate kiss and the danger he had made her feel. 'I'm twenty-three and perfectly capable of walking into a casino.'

'Yes, but you're very sheltered, Lucy. Not the kind of young woman who should be going into casinos late at night on her own.' Edward frowned with concern. 'You've spent your adult life working with children, for God's sake.'

She smiled. 'And looking after you and my father.'

'Well, all right,' he grinned, touching her face affectionately with one slim hand. 'Looking after me and your father.'

'And that is, after all, what I plan to do for the rest of my life,' she pointed out with a teasing smile.

'Yes,' he said softly, 'but don't go into that damned casino again. It just isn't suitable, my darling, and I won't allow it.' He bent his head to kiss her. The warmth of his mouth was sweet, familiar, and she smiled as she received his kiss, her body relaxed as he held her waist tenderly.

Suddenly she remembered the pulsing excitement of that man's kiss last night and her heartbeat started to race dangerously. Eyes darkening, she moved abruptly away, ending the kiss.

'If only we were married,' she said suddenly, a hand at her temple. 'Darling, can't it be soon?'

'It's so difficult, Lucy,' he said with deep regret. 'To even think of marrying yet could be disastrous.'

'But if we were married, you could live here instead of at that poky little flat,' she protested, 'and do something about Daddy. I sometimes feel as though I'm drowning in all this worry——'

Edward groaned, pulling her back into his arms. 'You shouldn't have to worry about things like bankruptcy and ruin,' he smiled teasingly at her. 'All you should worry about is darning my socks and cooking dinner for me and your father.'

Lucy clung to him, arms wound round his neck. 'It's all I want to do, Edward. Just to look after you and my father forever——'

'Then get on with the dinner,' he teased, kissing her, and then released her, opening the kitchen door. 'I'll be in the drawing-room with your father.'

As she prepared the dinner she listened to her favourite piece of jazz, the piano a smoky lilt against the lazy drawl of the singer. If only life could be this simple, she thought, green eyes clouding. Just relaxing, with no financial worries.

Sighing, she remembered how safe and secure her childhood had been. Sir Charles had been alive then, and his had been the strong hand that guided her life. If only she could return to that haven . . . but her father was at the wheel now, and guiding their ship on to the rocks.

The whole house felt under constant threat. She had no idea about raising money. What on earth did one do? Sell furniture? The paintings and jewellery that had not been sold so far would raise some money, but not enough. She only earned a small amount from the kindergarten. Enough to buy household necessities and food. But nowhere near enough to pay off a mortgage or even debts.

On Saturday morning she went shopping as usual, while her father slept off his hangover. It was a lovely day, the sun high in a clear blue sky.

As she walked towards the shopping precinct, a long white sports car slid around the corner and purred to a standstill just in front of her. The door opened and a very tall man stepped out of it, impeccably dressed, turning to face her with a cool smile.

Lucy gasped as she saw the blue eyes and the scar.

'Serendipity,' Randal drawled. 'I was just on my way to see you. I came to return this.' He handed her the white silk shawl. 'You left it in my office the other night.'

Flushing angrily, she snatched the shawl from him. 'Thank you,' she said tightly, and tried to move past him.

He blocked her path. 'I thought you might come back for it in person.'

'Why on earth should you think that?' Lucy's green eyes sparkled with anger. 'After your behaviour, the only reason I would have considered returning would have been to slap your face.'

'I take it the idea didn't prove irresistible?'

'No,' she said tightly, 'but it will if you don't get out of my way!'

He laughed, blue eyes moving over her with blatant insolence. 'You are passionate, aren't you? I've never met such a spitfire. How quickly that cool little face turns to fury.'

'I scratch, too.' she said, loathing him intensely. 'Remember?'

'How could I forget?' He turned his dark head, the scratch a faint red line along his tough jaw. 'Every time I look in the mirror, I think of you and your angry little face. I'd like to make you that angry again, Miss Winslow. In fact, I'd like to make you angrier still...'

Staring, she felt her pulses throbbing with sudden wild arousal, and her gaze seemed riveted to his hard mouth as she remembered that kiss and the violence of the response he had aroused in her.

'Have dinner with me tonight,' he said softly, watching her.

'No!' she snapped.

'Tomorrow night?'

'Never,' she said fiercely, and stormed past him.

He fell into step beside her, hands thrust in the pockets of his obviously expensive grey suit.

'You're annoying me,' Lucy said, refusing to look at him.

'Good,' he murmured. 'I enjoy seeing you lose your cool.'

'I could call a policeman, you know,' she said, quickening her step.

'He wouldn't have the same effect.'

Her mouth tightened. They were walking briskly on to the cobbles of the precinct. Shoppers streamed all around them. She was very aware of Randal's hard masculinity, that lazy, mocking smile and the black windblown hair. Several women shot him interested glances.

'Will you please stop following me?' Lucy said tightly.

'You'd be disappointed if I did,' he drawled.

'Let's put that to the test,' she said flatly, glaring at him through her lashes. 'Walk away in any direction, and see how long it takes for me to start wailing with disappointment.'

He laughed, then his eyes narrowed shrewdly and he drawled, 'You came to the casino to try and stop your father gambling, didn't you?'

The sudden change of conversation threw her. Shock flared in her green eyes. She didn't reply, but her step faltered, she bent her head and felt her face run with hot colour.

'He was in the casino every night this week,' Randal said lightly, watching her bent head with calculation.

'He enjoys gambling,' she said coolly, lifting her head to signify her indifference, which of course she did not truly feel. But she didn't want him to know how worried she was by her father's drinking and gambling.

'But you don't?'

She shrugged lightly. 'It's hardly my sort of thing.'

'A pity,' he drawled mockingly. 'I hoped you'd turn up again. Don't tell me I frightened you off forever?'

'You'd frighten anybody,' she said, throwing him a haughty look.

'Would I, now?' he murmured, watching her with a wicked smile.

Her heart skipped a beat. She didn't like the way he'd said that. Desperate to get rid of him, she turned, then walked quickly into a department store. Randal followed her. Scent assailed them from the brightly lit counters.

'Shopping for make-up?' he drawled beside her. 'You don't need it. You have a beautiful face and perfect skin.'

'How poetic,' she said sarcastically.

'When I first saw you, I noticed you weren't wearing make-up. It seemed incongruous in the casino. But you don't need it with those eyes, do you? They're like green fire——'

'I do wish you'd go away,' she snapped.

'I can't help myself,' he drawled, smiling sardonically. 'You fascinate me.'

'Well, you don't have the same effect on me.' She stopped by a perfume counter, turning to glare at him. 'Or hasn't that occurred to you?'

He looked down at her, unsmiling. 'Oh, yes. But it doesn't deter me.'

'Perhaps a kick in the shins would work better?'

'You really are a tempestuous little creature, aren't you?' he murmured. 'It's funny. I've always had two types of women. Can never decide which I prefer.' He looked her up and down slowly, drawling, 'Virginal blondes or tempestuous whores.'

She caught her breath at his insolence.

'I always dreamed of meeting a woman who was both,' he said softly. 'And I did the night you walked into the casino. You're an exciting combination of madonna and whore. I'm afraid I can't be stopped. I must have you.'

For a long moment, she just stood there, breathless and afraid, staring up into his ruthless face. What he had said was unacceptable. She was so shocked that she couldn't summon the anger to slap his insolent face because she simply had never been spoken to like this in her life, and the worst part was—she believed he meant every word he said.

'Let me buy this scent for you,' he drawled suddenly, picking up an expensive test bottle. 'It's my favourite. I'm sure it will suit you.'

Raising the bottle, he softly pushed a swath of her blonde hair back, his long cool fingers touching her naked throat, hearing her catch her breath as excitement shivered through her.

'I must find your pulse, my dear,' he murmured, and slid his long fingers down until they encountered the hot throbbing beneath her white skin. 'Ah,' he said softly. 'Unmistakable——'

'Take your hands off me,' she whispered, rooted to the spot, almost hypnotised by him.

He just smiled, and then she felt the cool spray of scent on her throat. It felt so intimate, so erotic. 'I'll have to find all your pulses,' he said under his breath, unsmiling. 'One by one. The heat brings out the scent. Did you know that?' His hands slid to her wrists, lifted them both. He studied the bluc veins, feeling the rapid thud at his touch. He sprayed each wrist. His blue eyes flicked to meet hers compellingly. 'When you're my mistress,' he said softly, 'I shall put scent on your body every night.' His dark head bent closer to her. 'At your throat... your ankles——'

Lucy broke away from him in a sudden fury. 'How dare you say such things to me? How dare you?' She was so angry she was shaking from head to foot, her pulses throbbing wildly. 'If you don't leave me alone, I shall scream, and then a store detective will come over and——'

'Let me buy you this perfume,' he cut in, unconcerned by her threat.

'No!' she snapped, rage in her green eyes. 'I loathe it! It will always remind me of you!'

'In that case,' he drawled, 'I shall buy you a very large bottle of it. You must keep it in your bedroom. Put it on before you go to bed. Then you'll always think of me as you undress.'

'Oh!' Anger burning her cheeks scarlet, Lucy turned on her heel and stormed away from him, unable to fight him verbally, aware that her only defence was just to walk away. She expected him to follow her.

Incredibly, he did not. As she stormed out of the department store, the scent clinging to her, she was still shaking with rage. How dared he do that to her in a public place! Touch her throat like that, spray this beastly scent on her pulses. As for telling her point-blank that he wanted her to become his mistress...!

She wished she had slapped his face. Unfortunately, her horror of public scenes was too great. Still, she thought as she shopped alone for the next hour, he had obviously got the message in the end, because he didn't show up again, and she was glad of that.

When she got home, her father was up, drinking black coffee and relaxing in the drawing-room in an armchair, his white shirt open at the neck and his grey trousers expensive.

'Morning, darling,' he said lightly as she came in. 'Have you been out shopping?'

'We needed some food for the weekend.' She bent to kiss his unshaven jaw, the pale stubble rough against her soft skin. 'I got some essentials, and something special for dinner tonight.'

'You are a sweetie.' He smiled lovingly at her. 'By the way—a package came for you. It's over there, on the coffee-table.'

Lucy glanced at the antique table, frowning. 'For me?' She picked up the square gift-wrapped box, tensing as she saw the bold black handwriting on it.

'A boy delivered it,' said her father. 'About an hour ago.'

Opening the package, she saw the gold writing embossed on white and trembled with rage as the large box of French perfume was exposed. How dared he! How dared he!

'Something wrong?' Her father was watching her face.

With an effort, she controlled herself. 'No...nothing at all.' She gave him a tight smile. 'I'll just go and make myself some lunch.'

Going upstairs, she stormed into her bedroom, through to the connecting bathroom, and ripped open the box, unscrewed the vast bottle of scent and poured it all down the sink.

Waves of delicious scent engulfed her. Expensive, sexy, classy, fresh... it permeated the bathroom, drifted inexorably into the bedroom, clung to the cream carpet, the floor-length beige curtains, the cream-gold bed...

For the rest of the day, her bedroom was an emporium of scent.

And Randal's arrogant, mocking smile filled her mind every time she set foot into her room. By nightfall, the whole of the upstairs of the house reminded her of those moments this afternoon and the dreadful, wicked, shamefully exciting things he had said.

It was enough to make her scream...

CHAPTER TWO

THE next day, Lucy was polishing the drawing-room when she saw the long white sports car pull up outside the house. Pulses leaping with fury, she froze, staring. It was eleven o'clock, a sunny day, and her father was still asleep. If she didn't answer the door to Randal, he would wake her father, and she didn't want that. She didn't want him to know that this dangerous man had taken such a fancy to her and was in hot pursuit. He didn't even know she had visited the casino that night. What would he say if he found out what had happened? She had asked Edward to keep silent on the subject. They had dined together last night, as always on a Saturday night, and he had gone home at midnight, aware that her father was once more at Marlborough's casino. But Edward could do no more to stop her father than Lucy herself could. He had told her he would go to the casino at some point himself to try to prevent her father from gambling. But so far, he hadn't done anything. Lucy was afraid to go there again, and the reason for her fear was currently getting out of that long white sports car, flashing dangerous blue eyes to the house.

Randal walked with that lazy arrogance to the door. He looked casually wealthy in black trousers and a black cashmere V-neck sweater. His black hair was pushed back from his hard forehead, his blue eyes hooded by those heavy eyelids.

Lucy moved away to the hall, light footsteps taking her to the front door before he could knock or ring or make any sound that might wake her father.

Wrenching open the door, she looked angrily into his face. 'What are you doing here?'

He smiled mockingly. 'I came to see you. What else?'

'Well, I don't want to see *you*. Haven't you got the message yet?'

'But you've answered the door.' Black brows arched coolly.

Lucy's face flushed a delicate pink. 'I didn't want you hammering on the door and attracting attention. This is a quiet residential square. The neighbours notice everything that happens.'

He surveyed her with amused insolence. 'Nothing to do with your father sleeping off last night's hangover, then?'

Lucy's colour deepened. 'I don't know what you mean!'

'He was in the casino until dawn,' Randal said coolly, his face unsmiling. 'He ordered a magnum of champagne. I doubt he'll surface much before lunchtime.'

'Gossip?' she queried, dislike in her green eyes.

He laughed under his breath. 'That's right. Aren't you going to ask me in? I'd love a cup of coffee.'

'No, I'm not going to ask you in,' she said tightly, and began to close the door.

'Want me to start hammering on the door?' he drawled, preventing her from shutting it with one strong hand.

Her eyes warred with his. Angrily, she felt she had no option but to let him in. 'Very well,' she said angrily. 'I'll let you come in. But one false move and I'll scream the house down.' Holding the door back for him, she felt her pulses leap as he moved inside.

He dominated the hallway, his presence like electricity. He was so tall—at least six feet four—and those shoulders were intensely broad, his body rippling with lean muscle.

Lucy looked up at him through her lashes. 'We'll go in the kitchen. Please keep your voice down...'

He followed her coolly along the hall. Lucy was so aware of him behind her that her pulses were leaping like fire by the time they reached the kitchen.

As they entered the sunlit pine kitchen, she turned and found him right behind her, very close, his muscled chest at eye-level, the tanned flesh visible where the V of his sweater ended, and a sprinkling of black hairs curling there.

Her eyes flashed to meet his. Their gazes collided with violent impact. She felt breathless suddenly, her heart thudding with alarm. Why does he affect me like this? she thought in panic.

'I'll get you that coffee...' she said, her voice oddly husky, and turned away from him, going to the side and switching on the kettle.

He moved behind her, and she felt his breath on her neck as he bent his dark head, long fingers pushing her blonde hair softly back to expose the naked nape of her neck.

'You're not wearing that perfume,' he said softly, and his mouth kissed her throat.

Angrily, she turned. 'Keep your hands to yourself!'

'Why aren't you wearing it? I went to a great deal of trouble to have it delivered here for you.'

'I couldn't stand the smell of it,' she said deliberately. 'It reminded me of you.'

'What did you do? Pour it down a sink?'

Her face flamed. 'Yes!'

He laughed. 'Well, that rebounded on you, didn't it? The whole house smells of it.'

'It'll go away eventually,' she snapped. 'Just like you.'

'But I won't,' he said under his breath, moving towards her. 'I won't go away until I've got what I want.'

She backed, found herself cornered, heart thudding as she stared up at him in sudden wild panic. 'But what is it? What do you want from me?'

His blue eyes moved to her mouth, then her full breasts as they rose and fell beneath the pale blue silk dress she wore, and they were both suddenly aware of the swift erection of her nipples as excitement shot through her under that powerful gaze.

'I want to make love to you,' he said softly.

It was suddenly impossible to breathe. Lucy stared at him, her body tense. As those blue eyes flickered back up to meet hers she felt her heartbeat rocket.

'Well!' She was almost speechless. 'If you think that I...' The words seemed to stumble over each other. 'That I would dream... think of... even consider...'

He was smiling sardonically, his strong hands moving to her waist as he took that last, deadly step towards her.

'Don't...!' she gasped out.

His hard thighs pressed inexorably against hers. He had her completely cornered now, her heart drumming as she clutched his powerful arms with nerveless fingers.

'Have dinner with me tonight,' he drawled. 'Or I'll kiss you until your legs give way.'

'I'll scream!' she whispered, appalled to realise that she was almost hypnotised by him.

'Then scream,' he mocked, and bent his dark head, very slowly, giving her time to scream her head off, but she couldn't move or speak as that hard mouth came closer, her pulses drumming feverishly as she waited for that kiss.

His mouth closed over hers at last, and she shook as his lips parted hers, a terrifying sweetness invading her body as she felt her mouth open beneath his and accept the hot exploration of his kiss. Pleasure was flooding her, her eyes closing and her hands curling on his broad shoulders, loving the feel of those firm muscles beneath her fingers. The kiss was slow, sensual and unbearably exciting, making her want more, her pulses clamouring as she suddenly felt an urge to touch his strong throat and push her fingers slowly through his dark hair.

With a smothered gasp of self-loathing, she struggled out of that hot embrace, but his arms tightened around her and his kiss deepened, his mouth forcing her to accept the growing passion of the kiss. She started to hit out at him, giving hoarse gasps of angry excitement as she felt that hard male body in every nerve-ending, and, most of all, felt the press of his manhood against her.

Suddenly, she was terrified. Her voice shakily pleaded for release. 'Please...' Her mouth was against his, her body trembling. 'Please let me go...Randal...' She felt humiliated, intolerably excited, confused...

He released her with reluctance, his mouth lifting from hers as though he could not bear to stop kissing her. He looked down at her flushed, fevered little face, saw the green eyes enormous with panic, the pulse beating hotly at her throat.

Lucy struggled away from him, backing across the kitchen.

'Do I get a dinner date?' he asked thickly.

'No,' Lucy said at once, and then, on a sudden inspiration, 'If my boyfriend catches you here, he'll kill you.'

'Boyfriend?' he said sharply, frowning, then as though to himself, 'Of course...' The black lashes flickered. There was a little silence as his mouth hardened. 'Who is he? How long have you been seeing him?' His eyes darted down. 'It can't be serious because you're not wearing a ring.' His eyes shot back to her face. 'Are you in love with him? No, you can't be or——'

'I have no intention of discussing my personal life with you,' she snapped heatedly, keeping her distance. 'Now kindly leave.'

'Are you in love with him?'

Her mouth tightened. 'You don't give up, do you?'

Randal laughed. 'Never. At least—not when I want something.'

'You can't have everything you want.' She lifted her chin, eyes defiant. 'Life isn't like that.'

'Perhaps not for other men,' he drawled arrogantly, 'but I can assure you it is for me. I always get what I want. There's always a way. Didn't you know that?'

'Not with me,' she said flatly. 'You'll never find a way to get——'

'I only have to find your Achilles heel,' he murmured, smiling. 'And I think I already have—don't you?'

She flushed, pointing suddenly to the door. 'Get out of here!'

He laughed, eyes mocking. 'That gesture would be more effective if you hadn't kissed me back so passionately just now.'

Fury shot through her. She abandoned her stance. 'I didn't kiss you back. I was cornered and forced into it.'

'You could have screamed,' he drawled, laughing at her. 'But you presumably wanted it as much as I did. What's the matter—doesn't your boyfriend know how to kiss?'

'How dare you?' she said, trembling with rage. 'He's ten times the man you are.'

'But he hasn't made love to you yet.'

'He's not like that,' she said heatedly. 'He wouldn't dream of——'

Randal laughed with such open mockery that she couldn't continue.

'I'm not discussing him with you,' Lucy blazed, hating him violently. 'Now please just accept that I don't want anything to do with you—and leave.'

He smiled lazily, hands thrust into black trouser pockets. 'I'm afraid I can't do that. I want you far too much.' He moved suddenly, striding towards her with coolly lethal sex appeal and making her back away, her heart in her mouth.

'If you kiss me again, I'll——'

'Don't worry,' he said softly. 'I won't kiss you again. Not just yet.' His hand touched her chin, cool fingers making her pulses race. 'I can hear your father moving about upstairs. I don't want to run into him. And you don't want me to, either—do you, Lucy?'

She flushed, jerking her chin from his grasp. 'I just want you to go. That's all.'

'The more you run,' he said softly, 'the harder I'll chase.'

Breathless, she stared into the powerful face. 'Why?' she asked in sudden overwhelming panic.

'Because I'm that kind of man,' he drawled sardonically, smiling with amusement at her fear. 'A hunter. A predator. I enjoy the excitement of the chase, and you're the most exciting prey that's ever caught my fancy.'

As she shivered, he turned coolly from her, a smile on his hard, mocking face, and left the kitchen, closing the door quietly behind him, his footsteps moving with panther-like grace to the front door.

Lucy was trembling as she sank into a chair at the kitchen table, the morning sunlight streaming over her through the windows, and heard the front door close behind him.

What on earth was she to do?

Edward arrived at three for Sunday lunch. Her father had been up for two hours, and was flicking idly through the Sunday newspapers in the drawing-room. Lucy had prepared most of the lunch and was just waiting for it all to be ready. The potatoes were roasting in the oven along with the lamb and the onions. Various saucepans filled with vegetables were bubbling on the hobs.

'Mmm!' Edward strolled over to the stove. 'Smells delicious! How long till it's ready?'

'Fifteen minutes.' She glanced at her watch, poked the carrots with a fork. 'You didn't go to the casino last night, did you?'

He grimaced. 'It was so late when I left——'

'Daddy was at the casino till dawn, drinking champagne.' She sighed heavily. 'Edward—somebody's got to do something. We must be running out of money. Surely you can——?'

'I'll go to the casino tonight,' Edward cut in smoothly. 'I promise.'

'Thank you.' She touched his thin shoulder gratefully. 'You see, I'm sure if one of us actually turned up there, he'd realise how serious our worries are.'

Edward raised blond brows. 'Don't bank on it, darling. Your father already knows. Turning up at the casino may have no effect at all.'

She felt so frustrated that she put her hands to her temples. 'What will we do when the money runs out——?'

'We'll get married.' Edward slid his hands on to her waist, smiling. 'And I'll give you all the security you need.'

Lucy went into his arms with a sigh. As he kissed her, she compared his soft, gentle mouth with the fierce excitement of Randal's kiss, and she felt suddenly angry.

She pulled Edward's head closer and tried to deepen the kiss, instil some urgent passion into it.

Edward jerked his head away, frowning. 'Lucy...!'

Humiliated, rejected, she stepped away from him, her face running with scarlet colour.

'Darling.' He sounded exasperated, running a hand through his blond hair. 'It's hardly the time or place...'

'Edward.' She lifted her head suddenly, emotions boiling to the surface after his rejection, her voice hoarse as she asked a question that suddenly demanded an answer. 'Do you love me?'

He stared, even more appalled. 'What a question! Of course I love you!'

'Then why don't you want to marry me until my father's ruined himself?' she demanded. 'Why are you waiting for that ear-splitting crash? Why won't you do something, Edward? Why do I constantly feel as though we're all just sitting in an aeroplane that's running out of fuel?' She moved towards him suddenly, green eyes blazing with anxiety. 'We're going to crash at any minute and nobody's *doing* anything!' Her hands curled on his lapels. 'Nobody's doing anything——'

'For God's sake, Lucy!' he whispered tightly. 'He'll hear you!'

She shook, closing her eyes, drawing an unsteady breath. 'Edward, I'm so frantic with worry.' Her eyes opened again, staring at him. 'I've known you all my life. You're the only person I can trust, rely on, turn to... but you're not *doing* anything, Edward—you're just waiting for the disaster that we can all see coming.'

'I'm trying to prevent it, Lucy,' he said flatly, and there was a sharp edge to his voice that she rarely heard, a cutting edge as though accusing her of something. 'I'm as worried as you are. More, if anything. But having you badgering me about it won't help.'

She looked away, flushing. 'I don't mean to nag——'

'But that's just what you're doing,' he said, eyes angry. 'Nagging at me and accusing me of doing nothing when I'm bending over backwards to try and stop this.'

'I'm sorry, Edward, I...' Guilt ran through her. 'I just feel so helpless...'

'Well, that's not surprising,' he said flatly. 'You are helpless.'

She looked up at that, astonished and hurt.

'You don't earn much money.' Edward counted her faults on long pale fingers. 'You're not qualified for anything more demanding than looking after three-year-old kids. You know nothing about finance or investment and you're hopeless at maths.' He raised his hands. 'What possible use are you to anybody?'

Silent, she just stood there staring at him as his words sank in. She felt as though he'd cut her off at the ankles.

Edward smiled and bent his head to kiss her cheek. 'You just stick with what you're good at, darling. You're far more help to your father and me when you're cooking our meals and keeping the house tidy.'

She did not dare reply in case she slapped his face. And the knowledge that she wanted to slap him shocked her even more than the insults implicit in what he had said.

'You serve the dinner, darling.' Edward smiled, pleased by her silence. 'I'll go and have a drink with your father in the dining-room...'

As the door closed behind him, Lucy was struggling to suppress the anger rising in her. He had never spoken to her like that before. Never. How dared he...anger burned at the back of her eyes...how dared he...?

Suddenly, she put her hands to her hot face in self-recrimination. Edward's right, she told herself again and again, but still that anger rose in her like a dark demon, and in the end all she could do to stop it bursting out was busy herself carving the lamb.

After lunch, Edward and her father fell asleep in the drawing-room. Lucy washed up. It took over half an hour. By the time she had finished, she was feeling an uncharacteristic burst of fury. Putting her head round the drawing-room door, she heard them both snoring. Edward was asleep in an armchair, a newspaper open beside him. Her father was asleep on the sofa, his mouth slack.

Quietly closing the door, she escaped upstairs. Her bedroom was filled with that damned scent. Prickling angrily, she opened a window, but it didn't help much. All she could think of was Randal: his hard insolent face, the ruthless mouth and the mocking blue eyes.

She remembered him spraying the scent on the pulse that had throbbed at her throat. She remembered the intimate eroticism of the act, and the way he had promised he would scent her wrists and ankles.

Lying down on her bed, she thought she was furious, but she wasn't... she was aroused. Her eyes closed and she remembered his hard body against hers, his hot mouth taking possession...

I hate him! she thought fiercely, sitting bolt upright on the bed. I hate him, I hate him, I hate him...! As for his boast that he always got what he wanted—he was in for a surprise. He could pursue her as much as he wanted—he would never catch *this* prey.

Three days later, her father got in at dawn and left a joyful, drunken note for her propped on the kitchen table.

'Guess what! We've been invited to the Mallory Ball!'

Lucy read the note with a frown as she made herself breakfast at eight. The Mallory Ball? The name rang a faint bell, but she couldn't place it, so she shrugged and went to work without giving it another thought.

When she got home that evening, she found Edward and her father drinking champagne in the drawing-room and laughing loudly while *Carmina Burana* crashed in fatalistic drama from the stereo.

'Darling!' her father laughed when he saw her. 'You shall go to the Ball!'

Lucy slid her jacket off, frowning. 'Yes, what is all this about?'

'The Mallory Ball, darling!' Her father turned the stereo down, smiling. 'Only the most important event in the social calendar. My word, I'm surprised you're not over the moon. Most young women your age would jump at the chance to go.'

'But what is it?' she persisted, sighing.

'It's a glittering affair,' her father said, 'held annually at Mallory Hall in Kent.'

'Look it up in Tatler,' Edward commented drily.

'Who invited you?' Lucy asked, impressed.

'That's the most exciting part.' Her father was beaming. 'Marlborough himself.'

'Marlborough?' Her eyes widened with dismay. 'The casino...?'

'The owner of the casino.' Gerald Winslow nodded. 'He also owns Mallory Hall—my God, he's one of the richest men in England. And he obviously likes me, or he wouldn't have invited me to his home.'

'He's a powerful man,' Edward said, smiling at Lucy. 'Owns a string of racehorses, several banks, and of course the casino. It's a real accolade for your father to be invited to this Ball, Lucy.'

'But it's not just me,' Gerald Winslow said proudly. 'The invitation was delivered personally to me by Marlborough himself, and it includes my family.'

'Shame I can't go,' Edward complained. 'Couldn't you pass me off as your son?'

'I wish I could,' Gerald sighed. 'But I don't dare. If he found out—well, I might destroy this sudden friendliness that's sprung up.'

'You're right.' Edward shrugged. 'Take Lucy. I'll be happy just to hear about it.'

'I shall buy you a new dress for the occasion, Lucy.' Gerald beamed at his daughter. 'Something superb...a fairy-tale creation...'

'No,' she said at once, paling. 'I have plenty of dresses good enough to wear.'

'We'll go to Harrods——'

'We can't afford it,' she said, horrified. 'Daddy, I don't even want to go to this wretched ball and——'

'You'll do as you're told,' her father said flatly. 'You must make a good impression on Marlborough. Edward—talk some sense into the girl.'

'All right.' Edward laughed, moving towards Lucy, taking her arm and leading her into the kitchen.

'You shouldn't encourage him like that,' Lucy said as he closed the kitchen door behind them. 'Making friends with the owner of that casino is just disastrous. Surely you can see——?'

'It's not disastrous,' said Edward under his breath, pale blue eyes fierce and his tone a warning note. 'It's the best thing that could have happened, and you mustn't interfere, Lucy.'

She stared at him, her lips parted. 'But——'

'No buts,' he said flatly. 'Don't do anything to jeopardise this friendship with Marlborough. I can't begin to tell you how vital this is. The invitation to Mallory Hall is a life-saver.'

'But how can it be when——?' she wailed.

'Just do it, Lucy,' he cut in angrily. 'Go to the ball, wear something fantastic, and make a good impression on the man.' He turned, opening the door, casting a brief, irritated look back at her. 'And get the dinner on, will you? I'm starving.'

Lucy suddenly wanted to throw something at his back as the door closed. Fury rose in her like fire. How could he speak to her like that? After everything she'd said about how worried she was, how frightened about her father's increasing gambling and drinking...to encourage him to go to this party.

Still, he had sounded earnest. Was it true that this friendship with Marlborough was the best thing that could have happened? And if so—why? It just didn't make sense.

The day of the ball dawned. Lucy changed into the fairy-tale dress her father had bought her, and shuddered at the thought of how much it had cost.

Made of ivory satin, it was off-the-shoulder, flouncing to a boned waist and flowing over hoops to the floor. She looked like a fairy princess in it, her blonde hair piled in loose curls on her head, the Winslow pearls that had been her mother's gleaming at ears and throat.

They drove to Kent in her father's Bentley. Lucy felt deeply disturbed by the whole affair, aware that her finery could vanish at any moment, just as this expensive car could, and the house, stolen by bankruptcy and ruin... If only her father would stop.

The gates of Mallory Hall were impressive white stone. A guard waved them through, an Alsatian straining at the leash, barking. The drive was long, winding, tree-lined. Lights suddenly loomed ahead, and the Hall came in sight, glittering rows of luxury cars parked outside it, the vast white Georgian mansion breathtakingly beautiful, worth millions, and looking every inch the home of a powerful man as it towered in strong masculine dignity against that moonlit night.

After parking, they walked along the gravel drive to the white stone steps. A butler greeted them, his face impassive. Jazz music floated from the lofty ballroom as he led them to it. Voices and laughter echoed in the palatial room.

'Mr Gerald Winslow,' intoned the butler, reading the invitation, 'and his daughter, Lucy.'

A very tall man with broad shoulders and dark hair swung to look at them, and Lucy gasped in horror, staring into that hard face, the insolent blue eyes, that scar jagged on his tanned cheek.

What was he doing here?

Suddenly, she realised that he must have received an invitation, too. Obviously, as he did work for Marlborough. He was striding towards them now with a mocking smile on his ruthless mouth, wearing an impeccably cut black evening suit.

'Glad you could make it, Winslow,' he drawled.

'Delighted, Marlborough.' Her father smiled, one hand moving to encompass a white-faced, appalled Lucy. 'May I introduce my daughter, Lucy? Lucy, darling—this is Mr Randal Marlborough.'

Randal was taking her hand in a powerful grip, mockery in his eyes, and as she stared into his handsome face she thought, oh, my God...he's Randal Marlborough...

'Charming,' Randal drawled, eyes sliding with cynical inspection over her body. 'Quite charming.'

Angrily, she flushed, deeply aware of her bare shoulders, the exposure of her breasts, the creamy swell highlighted by the exquisite décolletage of the dress, satin ribbons and lace surrounding her breasts and bare arms.

'Must say,' her father was beaming, 'this is an exceptional house. It's a listed building, isn't it?'

'Yes.' Randal smiled sardonically. 'But my equerry could tell you more about it than I. He really knows the history of the place. Let me introduce you...' He turned, eyes narrowing as he beckoned a well-dressed man across the room. 'Jamieson—this is Mr Winslow. He wants to hear about the house.' He took Lucy's arm, adding coolly, 'I'll get your daughter some champagne.'

Before she could protest, he was leading her across the vast ballroom, his face dismissive as he gave cool, polite nods to the people who clamoured for his attention, striding past them, his strong hand on Lucy's arm.

'What do you think you're doing!' she protested angrily as they reached the far side of the ballroom.

'Chasing my prey,' he said softly, and pushed open a door, hustling her into a lofty corridor of polished gold oak.

CHAPTER THREE

'WHY didn't you tell me who you were?' Lucy demanded. 'I thought you were the casino manager or even a croupier. It never occurred to me that you were Randal Marlborough.'

'Would it have made a difference to your response if I had told you?'

'No!' she said haughtily. 'I would still have found you the most loathsome man I've ever met.'

'Good,' he drawled. 'I'd hate to think you were only interested in my money.'

'I'm not interested in you at all!'

He laughed, eyes deliberately mocking.

'Why do you laugh at me continually?' she snapped. 'Do you think I don't mean what I say?'

'It amuses me to see you lose your temper. You're ice-blonde and fine-boned—a cool, classy young woman with aristocratic hauteur...' His eyes mocked her. 'When you're angry you turn into a ravishing green-eyed cat. I find it very exciting to provoke you.'

Her cheeks burned angrily. 'If I didn't find you so detestable, you wouldn't be able to provoke me.'

'No other man does?'

'No!' she flung at him, lifting her head.

'How very interesting,' he said softly, and Lucy felt her flush deepen, confused suddenly as she stared at him. He slowly let his blue eyes drift insolently over her naked shoulders. 'That dress is quite superb. I'd love to take it off.'

Fury blazed through her veins. 'You really are the most insolent man I've ever met!'

'Quite superb,' he said again, softly, and stroked the satin bodice with a long finger, adding lazily, 'I wonder your father could afford it.'

'What makes you think my father can't afford to buy me a new dress?' she demanded in a thickly choked voice, her green eyes blazing with angry pride and a tinge of fear.

'I merely meant that the dress is exquisite. I imagine it cost a king's ransom.'

She flushed, aware that she had almost betrayed her father's financial situation. 'I—I see...'

His cool hand took her chin, forced her head up. 'What did you think I meant?'

She paused, then lifted haughty blonde brows. 'Nothing.'

'Nothing at all?' he drawled mockingly, and a gleam in his eyes made her confidence waver, suddenly wary again as she felt a distinct stab of fear. Did he know her father was poised on the edge of bankruptcy?

'Where did you get that scar?' Lucy asked rudely, aware that it would end the conversation about her father and money.

'I wondered when you'd get around to asking me that.' He took her wrist, and opened a door. 'Come in here and I'll tell you.' With a tug on her hand, he had her inside the room and was closing the door, leaning his back against it.

Lucy backed away from him, green eyes wary. Glancing around the room, she saw they were alone. The room was a very big study in masculine colours of red and dark brown with a desk, Regency chairs and a long, deep, brown leather couch.

He pointed to the wall above the Georgian fireplace. 'That's my father. He didn't give me this scar, but it always reminds me of him.'

Turning, she saw an oil painting of a man. He was very handsome with black hair and penetrating blue eyes. He had a tough mouth and was dressed in an expensive black suit.

'Sir Henry Mallory,' Randal drawled beside her. 'I like to keep his portrait here. I look at it and smile because I'm master of Mallory now, and I like that.'

She turned to him, frowning. 'Didn't you get on with him?'

'I'm illegitimate. We only met a few times.'

Lucy was silent, her eyes watchful.

'Don't look so shocked, my dear,' Randal drawled. 'I'm not confiding in you. It's an open secret. I'm surprised you didn't already know.'

'I had no idea...' she murmured, glancing back at the man in the painting. He looked very like his father. That strong face, the arrogance and obvious powerful personality.

'I bought Mallory three years ago when he died,' Randal told her. 'The newspapers made quite a fairy-tale of it. Prodigal son and all that. I've never made a secret of my illegitimacy. If anything, I advertise it. It gives me a dangerous edge—just as this scar does.' He smiled lazily. 'I'm a great believer in using every natural gift as a bonus.'

Lucy looked up at him through her lashes. 'How did you get the scar?'

'At school. Someone made a remark about my parentage. A fight broke out. I fell through a plate glass window.'

'What school did you go to?' she asked, fascinated by his life.

'A hard one,' he drawled mockingly. 'And you?'

'A convent,' she said simply.

'Did you, by God?' He was staring at her mouth, her bare shoulders, the full breasts which rose and fell at the creamy satin décollatage of her dress.

'My grandfather sent me,' she told him, struggling not to respond to that hot blue gaze. 'And left provision in his will for me to stay until I was eighteen.'

'An astute man, your grandfather,' Randal said with a cool frown. 'He certainly knew what his son was made of.'

Lucy stiffened, green eyes flashing to his face. 'What do you mean by that?'

He smiled slowly. 'Nothing. And I'm tired of familial discussion. Time I stole that kiss...' His strong hands slid to her naked shoulders, pulling her towards him.

'No!' she gasped as her pulses leapt in wild response. 'Let me go!'

He laughed as she struggled, dominating her easily. 'Are you going to scratch me again?'

'Yes!' she snapped, hands flailing.

'You didn't scratch me the last time I kissed you.' He caught her wrists in strong hands, eyes mocking.

'I was too busy loathing and despising you!'

'Passionately?' he mocked, and his hands pulled her hard against his powerful male body.

She felt him in every inch of her, her breath coming faster and her heart pounding as he pressed her against him; and those rigid thighs, that hard-muscled chest, did terrible things to her.

There was an electric silence while he watched her unsmilingly. Then his dark head bent, and that hard mouth claimed hers, compelling a response. The powerful kiss made her moan softly as her mouth opened beneath his. The hot onslaught was irresistible, her heart drumming loudly as she found herself kissing him back, clinging to him, her slender body swaying in his arms.

Suddenly, he lifted her, his mouth still burning hotly over hers as he carried her to the long, dark brown couch, placing her on it gently, lying her on her back while he continued to kiss her deeply, and as her hands slid in shaking protest to his hard chest she felt his heart beating very fast, and that heavy excited thud made her own pulses clamour. She wound her arms around his strong neck, her mouth open passionately beneath his as he ravaged her senses with his kiss.

The door opened. They broke apart with reluctance, both staring towards the door. A woman in her fifties watched them. She had a Rubenesque quality: her body ripe and inviting, her red hair fading to gold-silver, her clothes elegantly sensual.

'Excuse me...' she murmured, closing the door.

'No, don't go, Mama,' Randal drawled thickly. 'I want you to meet Lucy.'

'I hardly think this is the time or place, Randal,' his mother said, lifting haughty brows. 'Miss Winslow is obviously at a disadvantage.'

'Then she will sink or swim,' said Randal, and got to his feet. 'Perhaps a glass of brandy will help her.' He strode coolly to the drinks cabinet a few feet away.

Lucy sat up, blushing furiously. She felt humiliated and dishevelled. Randal offered no help, and she loathed him for that. She got to her feet, lifting her blonde head and surveying his mother with as much cool dignity as she could muster under the circumstances.

'How do you do, Mrs Marlborough,' she said, head held high.

A smile touched his mother's mouth. 'How do you do, Lucy. Please call me Edwina.' Flicking green eyes to her son, she murmured, 'I don't think she needs that brandy.'

Randal smiled and said nothing, pouring the brandy regardless.

'You have a beautiful home,' Lucy said politely.

'Thank you.' Edwina glanced around the room. 'But the credit must go to Randal. He's stamped his personality quite firmly on Mallory.'

Lucy glanced quickly at the dark, exciting figure Randal was as he stood at the drinks cabinet. 'It's a very luxurious home.'

Edwina smiled. 'My son has a passion for luxury. His childhood, of course. They say deprivation is the mother of ambition.'

'You make me sound like Oliver Twist, Mama,' drawled Randal, strolling coolly back to them with a brandy, which he handed to Lucy.

'Hardly Oliver Twist, darling,' his mother said flatly. 'He didn't have women falling at his feet left, right and centre.' She looked at Lucy. 'Randal has a lethal effect on women. I do hope you're not going to join the ranks of the broken-hearted. He's left quite a wake.'

'I can assure you I wouldn't fall at any man's feet!' she said, tossing her blonde head. 'Let alone Randal's!'

'Quite true,' Randal said. 'She's more inclined to slap my face.'

Edwina laughed. 'How delightful!' She patted Lucy's hand. 'You're obviously a strong-willed young woman and nobody's fool. Randal has always been too attractive for his own good. Swooning women are so pointless. He needs someone strong enough to stand up to him. An equal. Someone not afraid to slap his face and tell him to behave.'

'I definitely don't approve of this conversation,' Randal said with a cool laugh, and took Lucy's untouched brandy glass from her, putting it on the occasional table. 'I'm ending it immediately.'

'I always say what I think, Randal.' Edwina arched a brow at him. 'You didn't expect anything less, did you?'

'I had some vague hope that you might tell her how charming and irresistible I am,' he drawled.

'Surely you've already told her yourself?'

Lucy laughed. 'Repeatedly!'

Randal took Lucy's wrist. 'We're going back to the Ball now. This is fast turning into the three witches. All we need is for the ghost of my grandmother to come floating out of the walls of Mallory with her cauldron.' He pulled Lucy with him to the door.

'Goodnight, Lucy,' Edwina called, watching with an interested smile.

'Goodnight, Edwina,' Lucy called over one bare shoulder as Randal led her to the door.

They left the room, going back into that lofty polished corridor.

'I liked your mother,' Lucy remarked as he led her down the corridor towards the ballroom, his strong hand possessive on her wrist. 'She's funny.'

'She's as tough as old boots,' he replied. 'A survivor from way back. If this was the Wild West, she'd be Annie Oakley.'

He pushed open the ballroom door and led her back into that glittering high-ceilinged ballroom.

'Randal, where have you been, *mio caro*!' A smouldering brunette with a throaty Italian accent and a revealing red ballgown intercepted them with a very dark look at Lucy. 'You haven't danced with me for ages. I insist you come and dance with me now.'

'Of course,' drawled Randal, giving a mocking half-bow to Lucy. 'Excuse me, Miss Winslow,' he said and he whirled the brunette away in his arms.

Lucy felt a sharp stab of jealousy which she irritably ignored. Walking across the polished gold oak floor, she seemed to glide, the satin ballgown glowing beneath the lights of the chandeliers.

She saw her father, and went to stand beside him. He was telling witty anecdotes to a group of people.

Staring across the ballroom, she saw Randal dancing with the sultry brunette.

'He's obviously lost interest in the blonde.' A voice floated to her from a group of people nearby. 'I thought gentlemen were supposed to prefer them?'

'Randal Marlborough is no gentleman,' a female voice said.

Lucy stiffened.

'The blonde was a fairy-tale princess . . . I suppose she gave in to him too soon.'

'That's always when he drops women,' the woman replied bitterly.

Lucy caught her breath. Angrily, she took a gulp of champagne, telling herself that she didn't care what they said. She thought of her passionate response to his kiss and her cheeks burned. No doubt he thought she was ready to give in to him. Fury made her eyes blaze. He could think again!

A shadow fell over her. Her eyes flew to the hard face as Randal bent his head and whispered in her ear, 'Come and dance.'

'No.'

He laughed. 'No polite excuses? And I thought we were getting on so well.'

Lucy glared at him. 'How many times do I have to refuse before you get the message?'

'You refuse my invitations,' he murmured, 'but never my kisses.'

Her cheeks burned. 'You can force kisses. You can't force invitations.'

'Is that so?' he said softly, eyes mocking her, and turned suddenly to her father. 'Winslow—that must be your fifth glass of champagne. Surely you won't be able to drive back to London tonight?'

Her father flushed deeply, saying, 'I... well, I...'

'Why not stay here?' Randal drawled. 'We have plenty of room and you don't need to be back early, do you?'

Lucy was appalled, her body rigid and her face chalk-white.

Her father was staring at Randal. 'That's very kind of you——'

'Think nothing of it,' Randal said lazily. 'You can return the hospitality some time. I shall be driving back to London tomorrow. Perhaps I could stop by for lunch?'

'We'd be delighted.' Her father stumbled over the words in his haste to accept. 'My daughter is an excellent cook and——'

'Thank you,' Randal interrupted, 'I'll look forward to it. In the meantime, I'll speak to the housekeeper and have your rooms made ready. Excuse me...' He moved away with a mocking smile directed at Lucy's furious face.

It had happened so fast. How had he managed it? She stood there, shaking, fury blazing from her green eyes as she watched him move around the ballroom with that cool arrogance, talking to people, occasionally dancing with a beautiful woman. There was nothing she could do or say to stop him, either. Anything she could have said would have revealed to her father the exact nature of her growing relationship with Randal Marlborough, and the thought of that was almost as appalling as the thought of staying here overnight. Apart from anything else—what would Edward say if he found out?

Later, Edwina Marlborough swept towards them, slender and beautiful on the arm of an austere silver-haired man in his late fifties.

'My dears,' she said with an amused glance at Lucy, 'I understand from my son that you're to be our house guests for the night? I've spoken to Mrs Travers. Your rooms will be ready in twenty minutes. I hope that's convenient for you?'

'Absolutely first class,' said her father, smiling broadly. 'Thank you very much, Mrs Marlborough.'

Across the glittering ballroom, Lucy saw Randal watching her with lazy mockery. Her temper flared. He thought he had her right where he wanted her. She could have screamed.

Soon, only half a dozen guests remained in the ballroom. Lucy had a sick feeling of excitement and fear in the pit of her stomach. The band were packing away, the caterers removing plates and glasses.

A tall, thin woman with black hair and a severe expression came over. Introducing herself as Mrs Travers the housekeeper, she led them out of the ballroom and into the palatial hallway.

They were taken up the sweeping staircase lined with portraits of past Mallorys. The family had owned the Hall since the eighteenth century, her father told her in a slurred, excited voice.

Mrs Travers stopped abruptly. 'Your room, Mr Winslow.' She opened a door, ushering Gerald in. 'Your daughter is directly next door.'

Lucy bade her father goodnight, then followed the severely dressed housekeeper. She was shown into a very lovely room furnished in cream and gold, the floor a mass of luxurious deep pile carpeting, the walls pale gold oak, the curtains floor-length cream velvet.

'Mrs Marlborough has provided you with night-attire,' said Mrs Travers. 'I expect it will be a size too big, but nevertheless comfortable.'

Lucy saw the cream silk nightdress and négligé on the bed. 'That's very kind. Please thank her for me.'

'I will, Miss Winslow.' The housekeeper left with a cool smile.

Locking the door immediately, Lucy took her ballgown off and laid it over a chair. The nightdress was a size too big, but fitted quite well for all that. Getting into bed, she felt able to sleep only because the bedroom door was so firmly locked. Randal might have been able to force this invitation on her, but he wouldn't get the chance to force any more of his unwanted kisses...

In the morning, she woke from a hot, sensual dream of Randal, his mouth at her throat while she moaned softly and ran her fingers through his black hair.

To find herself alone in a strange bedroom was a disappointment. For a moment, she lay there, staring around the room, feeling for the first time the emptiness of her heart. I have no one to share my life with, she thought, eyes darkening suddenly. No one to sleep with me, wake up with me, spend all his time with me.

Randal Marlborough flashed into her mind suddenly, and she saw with searing impact how it would be to turn and find him asleep beside her, his dark head on the pillow, his dangerous face softened by sleep.

Hot colour flooded her face. She tried to dispel the image, tried to summon Edward, but he was a pale comparison, thin where Randal was muscular, fair where Randal was dark, weak where Randal was strong.

Someone tried to open her bedroom door. She gasped, staring at the handle as it turned once, twice, then there was a silence.

There was a knock on the door.

'Who is it?' Lucy called, tensing.

'Your host,' drawled Randal's dark, sexy voice. 'Open the door and let me in.'

Lucy gave an angry laugh. 'I shall do no such thing!'

He laughed too, rich and deep, from outside the locked door. 'Darling, I admire your spirit, but I must insist you open this door.'

'You can insist all you like,' she said coolly. 'I shan't do it.'

'You want to eat your breakfast in a ballgown, do you?'

She hesitated, eyes darting to the ravishing satin dress lying on the chair near the bed.

'I've brought you a very attractive silk dress to wear instead,' Randal tempted softly. 'Open the door and I'll let you have it.'

That's what I'm afraid of, she thought. Then she frowned. She would feel ridiculous going down to breakfast in last night's finery.

'All right,' she said after a moment, and slid out of bed. 'Wait there and I'll be right out.'

Picking up her négligé, she dragged it on, belting it tightly at the waist with the wide silk sash. It was such a pretty set, white lace and intensely feminine. Barefoot, she padded to the door, blonde hair tousled and face make-up-free.

As she unlocked the door, she saw him leaning against the wall panel surround looking tall and excitingly attractive in an expensive grey suit. He seemed even taller now that she was barefoot.

'Well,' he said softly, blue eyes flicking over her slender body in the lace négligé, 'you really are something else, aren't you?'

Her pulses were already leaping. 'Is that the dress?'

Randal withheld it, supporting the flimsy pink silk on one strong brown finger.

Frowning, she tried to take it from him.

'Uh-uh.' His eyes glinted as he smiled mockingly. 'There's a price tag. And it's not money.'

Her lips tightened. 'I might have known there would be!'

'Well said. You never get something for nothing in this world.'

'So what's the price?' she asked, arching blonde brows, although she knew what it would be, and her legs were weak at the thought of it.

'A kiss,' he said. 'In private, freely given, and very passionate.'

Hot colour flooded her face. 'I'd rather eat breakfast in my ballgown!'

'Just one kiss,' he said equably. 'What's so terrible about that?'

'You know perfectly well,' she fumed, 'that it wouldn't end there. You'd want more, and you're not going to get it, so just——'

'I promise I won't demand more than you're prepared to give,' he cut in coolly, unsmiling, and made the pink silk dress dance on the end of his long finger. 'All I ask is one kiss in exchange for this dress.'

Her gaze fell on the beautiful silk dress. 'Where did you get it from, anyway? It looks terribly expensive.'

'One of my mother's,' he said. 'It'll be a size too big, I imagine, but there's something terribly sensual about loose silk on a slender woman's body. Especially a dress like this. I can just see it falling off your shoulders as you sip your coffee...'

So could she, and the image appealed to her newly awakening sensuality. 'All right,' she said on a reckless impulse, watching him through her lashes. 'One kiss—and no more.'

He moved into the bedroom, closed the door behind him, watched her from below his hooded eyelids, and suddenly the atmosphere was charged with a blazing excitement as she stood looking at him, her heart beating very fast, and her colour high.

Randal threw the dress on a nearby chair. 'Come here.'

Lucy watched him intensely for a second, then moved towards him. When she was very close, she stopped, her body almost touching his, and looked up into that dark, dangerous face.

'One kiss?' she asked throatily.

'A passionate one,' he murmured, eyes dropping to her mouth.

She moistened her lips with her tongue-tip. Slowly, she stood on tip-toe, her breathing accelerating as she put her hands on his broad shoulders, stared for a second at his hard mouth, then kissed him.

His mouth opened hers, his hands slid to her waist, he pulled her against him and she went willingly, fulfilling her side of the bargain with passionate pleasure, her arms twining around his neck and her fingers sliding into his thick black hair.

With a rough sound, he bent her backwards, and the kiss blazed into a desire she had never before experienced, her mouth sliding endlessly against his in hot exploration, aware of how slender and soft she was in contrast to the hard muscular power of the man who held her, kissed her so deeply, his hands sliding over the curves of her body.

The kiss blazed on and on. She was drowning, lost in a sensual dream, her heart like thunder in her ears and her legs quivering as she swayed in his arms, faint moans coming from the back of her throat. Her breasts were tingling with sensitivity against his hard chest, her whole body coming alive, and she wanted to stay lost, drown completely, her eyes closed and her head tilted back in abandon...

There was a knock at the door. For a second they did not acknowledge it, too lost in the kiss. Then Lucy's dizzy mind realised that someone was about to come in and catch her red-handed, so she dragged her mouth from his with a hot moan of protest.

'Randal...' She breathed his name, clinging to his broad shoulders, her legs so weak beneath her that she was afraid she might fall.

He was darkly flushed, staring at her with glittering eyes. 'Ask who it is,' he murmured deeply.

Lucy struggled to pull herself together. With a flash of accusation, she pushed away from him, her senses returning as she realised how completely she had given herself to him with that kiss.

'Who is it?' she called, trying to inject strength into her voice.

'Mrs Travers,' said the severe voice. 'Breakfast is being served in the dining-room, Miss Winslow. Your father asked me to let you know he was already down there.'

'Thank you, Mrs Travers.' Lucy put a hand to her hot temple. 'Tell him I'll be right down.'

The housekeeper's footsteps receded.

Lucy looked at Randal angrily. 'You must go at once. I have to get dressed and go downstairs.'

A hard smile curved his mouth. 'Unfortunately, you're right. I have a lot of work to do this morning before I accept your invitation to lunch.'

'You invited yourself,' she said haughtily, lifting her brows.

'That's the name of the game,' he murmured. 'You're my prey, remember? I'll use any means to trap you—fair or foul.'

'Usually foul! Not to say—loathsome!'

'Really?' he drawled, opening the door, mockery in his eyes. 'Your response just now was hardly disappointing. I look forward to closing in for the kill, Lucy. I can see it's going to be worth every moment of the chase.'

The door closed behind him, and Lucy stood alone, face burning. He had tricked her into that passionate response. She hated herself for giving it. Hated him for demanding it...

Refusing to dwell on her treacherous excitement for him, Lucy quickly took advantage of the luxurious connecting bathroom, took a quick shower and then dressed in the pink silk shift dress.

When she arrived in the dining-room, only her father and Edwina were there. It was a grand room with polished mahogany everywhere, a Jacobean fireplace of carved wood, and long, wide windows overlooking the dazzling green land of Mallory. Sunlight flooded into the room.

'Good morning, darling.' Gerald smiled at her, his eyes bloodshot. 'Did you sleep well?'

'Very well,' she said, smiling, and sat down at the long mahogany table. 'Thank you very much for lending me this dress, Edwina. It was very thoughtful of you.'

'Not at all.' Edwina looked marvellously bright and fresh, wearing a green dress, off-the-shoulder, voluptuous and bountiful. 'It was Randal's idea. He does have a thoughtful side to his character—despite the dangerous image he projects.'

The door opened and Randal entered, his presence dominating the room instantly. 'Good morning, everyone.' He sauntered to the table, kissed Lucy's cheek, then his mother's. 'Good party last night, wasn't it?'

'Wonderful.' Edwina patted her red hair. 'Poor James drank too much champagne and is sleeping off a hangover.'

'He's just not used to it,' Randal said, helping himself to kidneys. 'Has the ballroom been cleared?'

'Not yet,' Edwina said, 'although Mrs Travers is rapping out commands and terrorising the housemaids like mad to get it finished.'

Randal laughed, then flicked his gaze to Lucy, a gleam in the blue depths. 'That dress suits you, Lucy. I told you it would.'

Flushing deeply, she became aware that one flimsy silk shoulder-strap had slipped down to bare her shoulder completely, her blonde hair falling softly against her gleaming skin.

'What time do you expect to arrive for lunch, Marlborough?' Gerald Winslow asked, sipping black coffee.

'What time would be convenient?' Randal asked coolly.

'We normally serve lunch at three,' said her father.

Randal put his cup down. 'Three is perfect.' He got to his feet, magnificent in the grey business suit. 'I have to rush. I'll see you this afternoon.' As he strode behind Lucy's chair, he deliberately slid one long hand over her bared shoulder, murmuring, 'You must wear silk more often. It's incredibly sensual on your skin.'

Lucy's face burned scarlet and she lowered her lashes, pulses thudding. Randal left, closing the door and leaving Edwina and Gerald watching Lucy's bent head with amusement.

What can I do to stop him? she thought wildly. How can I make him leave me alone? He had forced her to stay here, forced her to accept that he would be coming to lunch today. What else could he force on her? And how long before she really was hunted down?

Edward flashed into her mind suddenly, so calm and gentle and kind. She felt waves of longing for his presence. He had been beside her all her life, as much a brother as he was a protector, not part of the family yet ever present, ever loving, ever supportive.

Edward would protect her if he knew what Randal Marlborough was trying to do. A sigh left her lips. How could she tell Edward? He would only be furious—perhaps angry enough to try to hit Randal. Irritably, she acknowledged the fact that Randal was the stronger of the two men. Not only was he at least six inches taller than Edward, but his body was built of pure lean muscle and he had a far more dangerous mind.

No, she couldn't risk Edward getting into a fight with Randal. Randal would humiliate and beat him effortlessly. So she couldn't tell Edward the truth about Randal.

But she could certainly make sure Edward came to lunch...

CHAPTER FOUR

WHEN Lucy got back to London, it was eleven-thirty. Her father went upstairs to shower and change, leaving Lucy in the kitchen to start preparing the chicken they had planned to eat today. When she had put the chicken in the oven and peeled the potatoes, Lucy washed her hands, dried them on a tea-towel, then telephoned Edward and invited him for lunch at three.

She chose to wear a sky-blue silk shift dress which she complemented with a long string of fake pearls and pearl-drop earrings. Blonde hair hanging soft and loose around her slim shoulders, she added a smudge of pale pink lipstick and was ready.

The doorbell rang as she was coming downstairs. Edward! she thought, and ran the last few steps to pull it open. 'Oh . . . !'

Randal stood on the doorstep, looking dangerously attractive. 'Not surprised to see me, surely?' he drawled with a mocking smile.

She was aware of her pulses leaping in response to his hard good looks. In the sunlight, that scar on his cheek made him look like a pirate.

She opened the door wider, stepping back. He strode coolly across the threshold, dominating the hall as Lucy closed the door behind him. Now he had spoiled everything! Edward wouldn't get here in time to be briefed about Randal. She could hardly whisper her plea for help over the luncheon table.

He was watching her, a frown on his hard face. 'Is something wrong?'

'Only the fact that you're here,' she said flatly, and tried to move past him.

His hand caught her wrist in long fingers. 'Come off it,' he said flatly. 'You were surprised to see me. And now you're lost in thought. What's going on, Lucy?'

'Nothing,' she denied guiltily, but her flushed face betrayed her.

The narrowed eyes probed hers shrewdly. 'You were expecting someone else...'

Her colour deepened. 'What of it?' she said defensively. 'This is my home; I can invite who I like.'

'And who do you like?' he drawled through hard lips, then an unpleasant smile tightened his mouth. 'Ah... of course... the boyfriend!'

His eyes were at once alarming and exciting, the blackness in their depths making her pulses throb and the hair on the back of her neck prickle upwards. Staring up at him, her mouth was dry.

'Well, well, well,' he said tightly. 'I wondered when I'd meet him.'

'He's coming at three,' she said, heart beating too fast.

'But how fascinating. I'll have a chance to study him at my leisure.'

The doorbell rang. Lucy tried to move to answer it.

Randal stopped her, eyes narrowed, hand biting into her wrist.

'I have to answer the door,' she said, trying to get away.

'And I have to remind you exactly who you're dealing with,' he said thickly, and then his head bent before she could cry out. His mouth closed over hers, and her puny struggles went unheeded.

The doorbell rang again.

Randal's kiss increased its pressure, refusing to let her go, though she wriggled, angry sounds coming from her throat. His hands moved through her hair, tousling it deliberately, arousing shivers of angry, inexplicable desire in her.

The doorbell rang a third time.

'Lucy!' her father shouted from upstairs. 'For heaven's sake—answer the door!'

Randal released her, mockery in his eyes. 'Yes—answer the door, Lucy...'

Breathless, dizzy, she stared at the mirror on the wall opposite, appalled at her reflection. Love-swept hair, bruised mouth, flushed face and fever-bright eyes.

'He's getting impatient,' Randal murmured as the bell rang again. 'I'll answer it for you, shall I?'

'No!' Lucy cried hoarsely, but he had already pulled open the door.

There was a stunned silence.

Edward smiled at Lucy as he saw her, then a frown clouded his handsome face and he stiffened, seeing her guilty flush, the glitter of her green eyes, the bruised lips, tousled hair... and the distance she stood from the door.

Suddenly, Randal stepped forwards from behind the door. 'Good afternoon,' he drawled. 'My name is Randal Marlborough. Won't you come in?' He behaved deliberately as though he were master of the house.

Edward stared at him in disbelief.

Lucy wanted to slap his handsome, mocking face. She'd never been so angry in her life.

Slowly, Edward walked into the house. Randal coolly closed the door, smiling lazily, sizing Edward up and finding him lacking.

Edward extended a hand. 'How do you do, Mr Marlborough. I'm Edward Blair, accountant to Mr Winslow.'

Randal's dark brows shot up. He shook hands with Edward, darting a narrow-eyed glance at Lucy. 'The accountant? How long have you been working for him?'

Lucy moved to Edward, one slim hand touching his shoulder. 'Edward has been with us for years,' she said softly, and stood on tip-toe to kiss his pale cheek.

'Years?' Randal's mouth hardened as he saw her deliberate gesture of intimacy with Edward.

'Yes, I don't know what we'd do without him.' Lucy ran a hand through Edward's hair, affectionately ruffling it.

'My father was accountant to Lucy's grandfather.' Edward kissed her cheek. 'When he died, I naturally took over.'

'Edward is practically an honorary Winslow!' Lucy added, smiling.

'Part of the family, then?' Randal said tightly, watching them.

'Yes,' Lucy said on impulse. 'We're going to be married.'

Randal's face turned to flint. 'Married?'

There was a tense silence. Edward was staring at Lucy in amazement and she flushed, unable to meet his eyes, aware that she had gone too far.

'How's lunch coming along?' a cheery voice called from the stairs, and the frozen tableau of three turned to stare as Lucy's father came down looking debonair. 'There you are, Mr Marlborough! Delighted you could make it!' He shook Randal's hand, beaming. 'Can I offer you a drink?'

'Thank you,' Randal said. 'A whisky would be appreciated. I've had a tough weekend. So damned busy...' He followed her father into the drawing-room with a cool stride.

Lucy cleared her throat. 'I'll go and finish the lunch.'

Escaping into the kitchen, she breathed a sigh of relief. Now that she had made it clear that she intended to marry Edward, perhaps Randal would leave her alone.

Edward came in as she was simmering the carrots. 'What on earth made you do that, Lucy?' he demanded, closing the door and walking to her.

'What?' she asked, blushing furiously.

'Announce our wedding as though it were imminent! I thought we'd agreed to wait.'

'No,' she said on impulse. 'That was what you wanted, Edward. You didn't really consult me at all.'

He was silent for a moment, taken aback. So was she. She had never been so direct before. She had let him dictate the terms of their relationship from the very beginning. But she couldn't any more. Not now that she was under threat from a predator like Randal Marlborough.

'I assumed you were happy with the arrangement,' Edward said slowly.

Lucy gave a deep sigh, putting a hand on his arm. 'Oh Edward, you know I love you, and I'm prepared to wait, truly I am. It's just that...' she moistened dry lips, 'I—I need some confirmation that I'm not waiting in vain. I'm twenty-three now, Edward. I've never had any other boyfriend but you and I...' she broke off, flushing as she whispered, 'I think I'm beginning to doubt you.'

He stared. 'Lucy, what are you saying?'

'That I'd like us to get officially engaged,' she said, amazed at her own boldness, but feeling pushed into it by Randal.

Edward drew a sharp breath, moving away from her. Lucy felt the pain of rejection, her hand dropping from him as he moved. He walked to the kitchen windows, hands in trouser pockets, and stared out at the small garden.

'This is all tied up with Randal Marlborough, isn't it?' he asked suddenly.

Lucy flushed deeply. 'You've been saying you'll marry me for——'

'Just answer me, Lucy,' Edward said flatly, turning. 'Marlborough's behind this somewhere, isn't he?'

She looked away, not knowing how to reply.

'He was kissing you when I arrived,' Edward said. 'Don't deny it. I'm not blind. I saw the tell-tale signs on both of your faces——'

'Edward...' She moved to him. 'You can't believe that I'd——'

'Oh, he's a very big fish to catch!' Edward cut in angrily. 'All that money, all that power—he'd certainly reinstate the Winslow family, wouldn't he? If you were Mrs Randal Marlborough, every door in London would be open to you!'

She recoiled from him in horror. 'If that were true, I would hardly have invited you for lunch to cramp my style and spoil my chances with him! I would deliberately have excluded you!'

He studied her for a second, his face pale. Then he looked away, saying, 'That's true...'

She breathed a sigh of relief. 'Oh, darling.' She moved to him again, her hand on his arm. 'I need you to make our engagement official. I need a ring... Edward, if I had a ring he'd leave me alone, I'm sure of it.'

He studied her, frowning, then said carefully, 'All right. We'll get engaged officially. I'll take you to buy the ring next weekend. I promise.'

'Oh, Edward...' she whispered, lifting her blonde head, tears in her eyes. 'Thank you.'

He smiled briefly and dropped a kiss on her mouth. 'But no weddings yet, Lucy. This is just an engagement. Got it?' Then he moved away from her, saying, 'I'll be in the other room, darling. You finish the lunch and don't worry.'

As he left, Lucy stared at the closed door, bewildered. They'd just got engaged—surely he should be rapturous, kissing her passionately? A thought flashed into her mind—did Edward really love her?

The question seemed horribly disloyal, and she angrily pushed it from her mind, but it wouldn't be vanquished, and as she went into the drawing-room, she met Randal Marlborough's dark eyes and felt excitement shoot through her like adrenalin. She could not deny her physical response to him. But she shied away from comparing it with her response to Edward...

They ate lunch in an atmosphere of tension. Lucy found herself seated next to Edward, opposite Randal, and Randal was icily polite.

'This is very good,' Randal said coolly as he ate the roast chicken. 'Thank you. Exactly what I needed after a hectic morning.'

'What made it so hectic?' Gerald Winslow asked, smiling.

'I've been to Newmarket to inspect a new yearling.' Randal sipped a glass of chilled Chablis. 'Then to the casino to check on the weekend accounts.'

'Don't you ever take any time off?' Edward asked sourly.

'Not unless there's something better to do,' he replied. 'I work hard and I play hard.'

'That's why you're so successful,' Gerald put in smoothly.

'Precisely,' said Randal with a wry smile. 'Besides—where money is concerned——' he looked back at Edward and gave a cool smile '—I don't trust accountants.'

There was a little silence.

'Oh?' Edward asked tightly.

'I never give them the chance to juggle the books,' Randal drawled softly. 'Particularly not when I've told them I'll be hosting a ball and drinking too much champagne. That's exactly the moment they're likely to rip me off.'

Edward flushed angrily. 'You must employ crooked accountants. We're not all like that, I assure you.'

'The only accountant I trust,' he drawled, 'is the one I've just checked up on and found innocent.'

Gerald Winslow laughed. 'Well, I admire your hard-headed business attitude, but I'm afraid I'm hopeless at figures. I have no choice but to trust my accountant.'

Randal smiled slowly, eyes pinning Edward to his chair. 'How very interesting.'

Lucy brooded for the rest of lunch, hating Randal for his deliberate insinuations. He didn't even know Edward. How dared he make such blatant statements?

It's just because he wants to poison Edward in my eyes. He's trying to make me stop loving and trusting Edward. Talk about ruthless! Was there nothing Randal would not stoop to?

After lunch, Lucy made coffee, took it in to them, and excused herself with cool politeness. At least if she washed up in the kitchen, she wouldn't have to listen to any more of his insults and insinuations.

The door opened fifteen minutes later, and she turned to see him in the doorway.

'Yes?' she asked flatly, looking him up and down.

'I wish you'd say that to me more often,' he drawled mockingly.

'What do you want?' she demanded, turning her back on him.

He closed the door, walking towards her as she stood at the sink. 'I'm leaving shortly. I have to drive back to Newmarket to put in a bid for that yearling.' He stood close to her, hands thrust in grey trouser pockets. 'I came to thank you for lunch.'

'I didn't invite you,' she shrugged, washing the last saucepan. 'It makes no difference to me.' She ran the saucepan under the hot tap to cleanse it of bubbles. It shone. She put it on the draining-board, picked up a tea-towel, dried her hands.

Turning, she gasped, finding him right behind her, standing so close his body almost touched hers, and the *frisson* of excitement that leapt through her was electrifying.

Hot colour surged up her throat and face. There was a brief, bitter silence. 'Don't try to kiss me, Randal,' she heard her voice say, almost hoarse. 'My boyfriend is in the other room—remember?'

'Was he jealous,' he drawled, 'when he realised I'd been kissing you?'

'Of course,' she said, flustered by his nearness.

'How jealous was he, Lucy? And how angry? You don't look to me like a woman who's been passionately kissed since Edward arrived. I've been watching for signs, but of course——'

'Edward and I aren't like that,' she snapped, hating him. 'I've told you that before.'

'So you have,' he drawled. 'And the more I get to know you, the less it makes sense. He professes to love you. But I'll bet he hasn't even tried to take you to bed yet.'

Her eyes flashed like green fire. 'Get out!'

'If he'd made love to you,' he murmured, 'you wouldn't respond so fiercely to my touch. But you're going insane with frustration, aren't you, Lucy?' His eyes slid to her mouth, his voice taunting. 'You can't help yourself...you go up like a touch-paper whenever I kiss you——'

'Get away from me!' she whispered, heart thudding with abrupt violence.

His hands slid down her shoulder, evoking shivers. 'You're an unexploded bomb waiting to be detonated. The thought of how that sexy, greedy body of yours will respond when I get you into bed is enough to take the roof of my head off.'

'If you ever try to kiss me again, I'll show you just how much I detest the sight of you!'

'I'll enjoy making you eat your words.'

'And I'll enjoy making you eat yours!' She struggled not to show her excitement. 'Edward's buying me a ring next week. Our engagement is official. He told me so——'

'It wasn't official before?' he cut in shrewdly, frowning.

Lucy flushed scarlet, feeling sick as she realised what she had inadvertently told him. 'I—I mean——'

'He made it official today when he realised he had competition,' he guessed, eyes narrowed and hard. 'Well, well, well. The more I hear about this passionate love-affair of yours, the less I like it.'

'Shut up!' she said hotly, trying to struggle out of his grip.

'What do you see in him?' His upper lip curled in a sneer. 'A fiery temptress like you. He's a milksop. Certainly no match for that temper of yours.'

Stung, she said, 'I don't even have a temper!'

He laughed in her face.

'It's true! I only lose my temper when you're around! You make me so furious I can't control myself! You make me want to——' She broke off with a hoarse little gasp, staring into his mocking face.

'Don't say another word,' he said thickly. 'Just do it.' And then his mouth closed over hers in a brief, searing kiss that made her head spin.

'No...' she moaned in rising madness against his hot mouth.

'Oh, yes...' he said thickly, hands sliding to cup her breasts and make her gasp and stare wild-eyed. 'Show me, Lucy. Show me just what I make you want to do!'

Heart pounding, she felt a reckless urge to do just that, and it flared in her as his hard mouth closed over hers, making her wind her arms around his neck and kiss him fiercely. He made a rough sound of excitement, arms tightening around her. His hard body pressed further against hers and the excitement swept her off her feet, her hands moving to his hair, tangling hungrily in it, her mouth open passionately beneath his. Danger and desire flooded her veins as she found herself unable to resist that kiss, that mouth, those long hard hands as they moved over her body, making her moan, suddenly aware that she needed this, hated him, hated herself, but needed it, this total blanking out of everything in life, everything but that hard, compelling mouth on hers...

When he released her, she was gasping for breath, her heart beating so violently that she was shaking.

Desperate to prove she hated him, she deliberately wiped his kiss away with the back of her hand.

'A passionate gesture,' Randal drawled mockingly. 'In keeping with your temperament.' He stroked one long finger over her mouth, smiling lazily. 'I'll buy that yearling and call it Miss Lucy's Passion.' He turned and strolled coolly from the room.

The door closed behind him, just as she was tempted by sheer rage to throw one of the saucepans after him. How dared he come here and insult Edward, make vile insinuations, force her to accept another of his hateful kisses? Certainly she wouldn't let him drip poison in her ear about the man she loved and wanted to marry. Edward had been her betrothed since the day she was born. Nothing could prevent her finding happiness with him. Nothing and nobody—not even Randal Marlborough.

The next day, Lucy spent a fun-filled but exhausting day at the nursery, looking after all the three-year-olds, who had spent the weekend with their families and were like mad dogs let off the leash, running around pouring paint over each other and trying to bury Lucy in the sandpit.

Walking home, she wondered how many children she would have. A long white sports car pulled up slowly beside her and her heart missed a beat. It shot ahead, stopped, and Randal stepped out. Lucy angrily tried to walk past with her nose in the air, but he blocked her path, forcing her to look up the expensive black business suit to his wicked, mocking smile.

'What do you want?' she demanded crossly.

He smiled. 'I bought the yearling. I wondered if you'd like to come and see it.'

Interest sparkled in her green eyes. She was very tempted, watching him through her lashes, knowing she wanted to accept the invitation, knowing also that it would lead her to dangerous waters.

'We'll drive down to Newmarket now,' he told her with customary arrogance.

'No,' she said flatly, 'I have to get home. My father will be expecting me and——'

'He won't,' Randal drawled with a lazy smile. 'I've already been to your house. He gives his blessing and hopes you have a lovely time.'

'What!' She stared at him, shocked.

'He's very keen that we should be friends,' Randal murmured. 'It would upset him if you refused my overtures.'

Her face coloured. 'That's blackmail!'

'Exactly,' he drawled and took her hand. 'Now get in the car.'

'I will not!' she said, temper rising.

'I'll pick you up and put you in if you don't.' Randal arched a cool brow, unsmiling suddenly, and as she looked at him she felt a quiver of fear, aware again of his powerful determination and how uncompromising he was when he wanted something. He simply went ahead and took it, knocking obstacles out of his way.

Her lips tightened. 'I'm not dressed for it. I've been at the kindergarten all day and——'

'I think you look lovely,' he said softly, blue eyes moving over her faded blue jeans and little blue camisole top. 'Besides—I want you to do as you're told. Get in the car and stop arguing. This excursion has paternal approval—remember?'

Lucy flushed angrily, aware she was trapped. 'Very well. I'll come to Newmarket with you. But only because you've made it impossible for me to refuse.'

She got in the car and they drove down to Newmarket. It was four o'clock, a sunny day, and, as they left London behind, Lucy began to enjoy the drive. Randal was relaxed at the wheel, his mouth a cool smile of triumph. Bach lilted through the car like pure sunlight.

Randal owned a vast stable on the outskirts of the racing fraternity in Newmarket. Large wrought-iron gates kept people out. A guard occupied a gatehouse and the stone walls surrounding the land were littered with barbed wire and broken glass. Various red signs threatened all sorts of awful fates if anyone tried to break in.

'You're very hot on security, aren't you?' Lucy commented, casting him a curious little look through her lashes.

'My horses are worth a lot of money,' he said coolly as they drove in through the gates and approached the stable complex of buildings. 'Several of them have won major races this season.'

He parked the car, and they got out. The main house rose before them in old red stone. Stable blocks were everywhere, surrounded by fields. Birds were singing in the late afternoon sun; the air was fresh and clean.

'This way.' Randal took her wrist, leading her across the yard towards a stable block. The scent of horses was intoxicating. A few trainers stood at the other end of the block, talking. They jumped as they saw Randal.

'Mr Marlborough, sir.' An Irishman in jodhpurs and bodywarmer came over to them. 'We didn't know you were coming today, sir...'

'Spur of the moment, Heaphy,' Randal said coolly. 'Bring Miss Lucy's Passion out, please.'

'Right away, sir.' He moved away to the seventh wooden door, opened it and clicked his tongue softly while leading out a magnificent yearling.

Lucy stared at it with rapturous eyes. 'Oh, it's beautiful...'

'He,' Randal drawled wryly, and stepped forwards. The yearling was jet-black, its coat rich and silky. Randal patted its strong muscled neck. 'He needs a little breaking in, of course. High spirited...just like his namesake.'

Her vanity was aroused. 'Are you really calling him Miss Lucy's Passion?'

'Of course,' he said coolly. 'But I can assure you I wouldn't have paid cold hard cash for an indulgence. His father was Black Jake. He won the National four times in a row. If his colt doesn't win every major race, I'll want to know why.'

'Oh, he's a fast one, sir,' Heaphy said at once.

Randal smiled with satisfaction. 'Blood always tells.' He patted the yearling again, then stepped away. 'Thank you, Heaphy. I'll drive down later in the week, check up on him.'

'Right you are, sir.' The Irishman tilted his cap with respect.

Randal turned and led Lucy away again. 'Shall we have some coffee before we drive back to London?'

'Why do you even bother to ask?' Lucy gave him a cool look. 'You never take any notice of my refusals.'

He laughed as they walked out of the stable block, into the sunlight and fresh air. The scent of horses permeated everywhere. It occurred to her that Randal had many different lives. This atmosphere of nature and fresh air was utterly opposite to the sophistication of the casino.

They went into the main house, and Lucy looked around at the open-plan design with surprise. It was so unlike Mallory. The room they stood in was at least fifty feet long, very bright and modern, rather like an expensive French farmhouse with its stone walls and cavernous ceiling, stark masculine furniture in beige and brown and a circular staircase moving up at the left.

'Do you live here?' she asked him later, as they stood in the bright, modern kitchen.

'Sometimes,' he drawled.

'So you have three homes?'

A cool smile touched his hard mouth. 'I have a low boredom threshold. If I spend too much time at the casino, I start to yearn for wide open spaces and green grass. If I spend too much time here—I start to yearn for sin and sophistication and glamour.'

'And Mallory?' she asked, excited by his words.

'Mallory's my base,' he drawled. 'It's also home. Home in a way no other place could be. There are generations of my family there. In paintings, plaques, books, memories—even ghosts.'

Her brows rose. 'Ghosts!'

Randal laughed, leaning lazily, hands in trouser pockets. 'There are several ghosts at Mallory. My favourite is Lord Anthony Mallory. He was the Highwayman. He had a secret passage built, leading from his bedroom to the stables.'

'Is it still there?' she asked, round-eyed.

'Oh, yes.' He nodded coolly. 'Remind me to show you some time. I used to explore it a lot when I first bought the house. I used to go around looking at the portraits of my ancestors all the time. It strengthened my sense of Mallory blood, put me in deeper touch with my true family.'

Lucy studied him, then heard herself say slowly, 'Did you know my grandfather was illegitimate?'

There was an acute silence. Randal put his cup down, not looking at her, and said coolly, 'Yes, I knew that. His natural father was an Earl, wasn't he?'

Lucy nodded, studying his tough face through her lashes. Suddenly, she felt overpoweringly aware of him. Her pulses were leaping, and she was tongue-tied.

To try and break the silence, she said lightly, 'Do you know, I've been in this room for five minutes, and you haven't said one thing that's made me want to hit you yet.'

'I must remedy that,' he drawled, flicking those wicked blue eyes to meet hers.

'Oh, no, please don't!' she said, lifting haughty blonde brows. 'It's such a refreshing change not to feel on the edge of explosion.'

'I must unquestionably remedy that,' he said darkly, moving towards her.

Lucy backed, heart thumping. 'No, you don't!'

'But that's what I want,' he said softly. 'To push you to the edge of explosion and then detonate you.'

Her breath caught as he reached for her, and then she darted away, evading his hard hands. Running out into the corridor, she saw a door and thought it might lead out to the garden. Pushing it open, she stumbled in, breathless.

Too late, she realised it was a bedroom.

'Oh . . . !' Staring at the long, low double bed dominating the vast wood and stone room, Lucy's heart began to thump with abrupt violence. She spun to face Randal as he entered the doorway.

'Good choice,' he drawled mockingly, and closed the door.

Quivering with sudden fierce desire, she angrily fought it, saying, 'I had no idea this was a bedroom!'

'Instinct brought you here,' he said softly, walking towards her.

'Don't be ridiculous!' She backed, heart thudding. 'Let me out at once!'

'You don't want to leave,' he said, advancing.

'I'm only twenty-three!' she said fiercely. 'I'm innocent and untouched!'

'And dying of frustration.'

Her legs hit the back of the bed. She fell backwards on to it, heart thumping, staring up at him with blazing, greedy eyes as waves of intense need flooded her body at the sight of him standing over a double bed looking down at her like this.

CHAPTER FIVE

RANDAL watched her in silence for a long moment, his face very close. Lucy felt as though she was looking into his eyes for the first time.

'Lie back on the bed,' he said under his breath.

Lucy just stared at him, her heart beating very fast.

Suddenly, he shouldered out of his jacket. Lucy's breath caught sharply. He threw the jacket to the floor and began to unbutton his tight black waistcoat.

'No!' She leapt away, but he caught her by the wrist and jerked her back as though she were a rag doll, suddenly making her aware of his real strength for the first time. Landing on her back, she sprawled, breathless, staring up at his dangerous face.

'You've wanted this for a long time,' he said under his breath.

'No...'

'Alone in a bedroom with me,' he said softly, eyes dark with desire. 'I see it in you, Lucy. You're going out of your mind with frustration.'

'It's not true!' She was shaking, her blood pulsing hotly. 'It's not true...'

His head moved closer, his hard mouth inches from hers. 'Don't you ever want to scream, Lucy?'

Her eyes closed. She shuddered. 'No...'

'Don't you ever want to break things?' he whispered, and his mouth was suddenly against her throat, sliding along the naked white skin tormentingly. 'To scream and smash that kitchen apart and tell those two men who guard you to let you live your own life?'

'Oh, God...' she whispered thickly, her hand clutching his head as intolerable need pulsed through her. 'Don't...'

His mouth moved back to hers. 'Your body needs love. It's clamouring for a man's touch. I can feel it. So can you. Give me your hand. Listen to your own body...listen...' He took her hand, raised it to the throbbing pulse in her throat. 'You want me...say yes...give in to your own desire...'

She moaned, lips parting, staring up at him, blood pounding in her ears as she stared at his hard mouth, felt her breath come faster, waves of desire flooding her.

'You always respond,' he said thickly. 'Every time I kiss you, touch you. Then you pull away, end your own pleasure. Why?'

'Because I hate you!' she whispered, staring at his mouth.

'No. You're punishing yourself. Refusing to give yourself what you need. Like a starving woman refusing food.'

'It's not the same thing!' she said thickly, shaking with desire, hands on his broad shoulders.

'Yes, it is, Lucy.' One strong hand stroked slowly down to cup her breast, his blue eyes watching her with dark, ruthless intent as he slowly circled his fingers over her breast, and her erect nipple thrust out in stark excitement as he stroked it tormentingly.

'Don't, don't...' she whispered. 'Oh...don't...'

He did not stop; his fingers were unbearably exciting, his face hard.

Suddenly, Lucy gave a hoarse moan of need, and was pulling his dark head down, lifting her face, her mouth passionately parted, and as his lips met hers they fell back together on the bed, the kiss blazing into a reckless fire of intolerable sweetness.

Her hands were in his hair, stroking the strong neck, and suddenly she found her fingers sliding over his dark red silk tie, sliding down to the unbuttoned black waistcoat that hung loose round his taut muscled chest.

She felt him push the silk camisole slowly, slowly up until her breast was bared to him, and as she felt his hand on her naked flesh she completely lost control.

Mindless, drowning in pleasure, Lucy tugged his tie and a second later he was loosening it with deft fingers, throwing it to the floor, and she kissed him with uncontrollable passion as she unbuttoned his white shirt to the waist, and buried her face against that hard-muscled hair-roughened chest.

Randal gave a harsh sound of excitement, and clutched her head to his bare chest. 'Oh, yes... yes...' His heart was slamming violently as Lucy's hot mouth crawled over his flesh. Lucy tore his shirt wide open, explored his torso with her hands and mouth, totally engrossed in her discovery of his body and her own excitement in touching him.

With a groan, he moved from her, tilting her head back as he slid his own mouth to her breast, stroking her with long fingers. She moaned and whispered his name. His tongue slid out over her nipple. Lucy arched against him, gasping, 'Oh, yes... yes... yes!' and his mouth came back to hers, their kiss blazing higher, tongues and breath mingling in erotic intensity.

When he tugged the silk camisole over her head she knew she should stop him, but she couldn't...she wanted him to touch her, wanted to feel those hands on her nakedness, and the pleasure as his hands rubbed her breasts was beyond endurance.

Their naked torsos met as Lucy gave a thick, hoarse cry of sheer pleasure, moving wantonly against his hard hair-roughened chest, her aching breasts rubbing against him in instinctive need. His mouth closed shakingly over hers, and they were both gasping, pressing together, their bodies tangling on the bed in a mêlée of thudding hearts and hot flesh.

Suddenly, he dragged his mouth from hers and he was deeply flushed, his breath coming in ragged gasps, his strong hands gripping her jean-clad thighs as he stared down at her wanton semi-nude body.

'We must stop now,' he said thickly. 'Or I won't be able to stop.'

Lucy stared at him feverishly, dazed and shaking from head to foot. She could barely move, let alone speak. She felt like a quivering mass of jelly. Nothing that had ever happened to her had prepared her for the engulfing passion she had just experienced.

'Did I prove my point?' Randal asked suddenly, watching her with narrowed glittering eyes.

Bitterness flashed in her passionate eyes. 'Yes...!' She raked one hand down his chest, black hairs crinkling beneath her fingers as she felt his hard thudding heartbeat. 'Oh, yes, you proved your point! But I still hate you for it!'

'Hate me, then!' he drawled cruelly. 'You still gave me what I wanted, and I only wish Edward were here to witness your fall from grace.'

The words were almost a physical blow. She stared in shock as the colour drained from her face.

Randal laughed, enjoying her pain. 'And you profess to love him!' He moved away from her, getting off the bed, smiling cruelly as her appalled eyes watched him start to button up his shirt.

Appalled, she crossed her arms in front of her naked breasts, whispering, 'My God... you swine... you did that deliberately to make me——'

'I didn't make you do anything, Lucy,' he said flatly, knotting his tie. 'You did it all by yourself.'

Rage flared in her eyes. 'You know I wouldn't have done that if you hadn't——'

'All I did was kiss you,' he said, arching black brows as he buttoned his black waistcoat. 'You did the rest. And very nice, too.' He laughed with cynical mockery. 'You really let the genie out of the box, didn't you? Good girl. I knew you had it in you.' He picked up his jacket, turned on his heel, strode to the door and unlocked it. 'I'll be in the car,' he said over one broad shoulder. 'Come out when you're ready to face me and I'll drive you home.'

The door slammed behind him and Lucy knew she had a choice: either she collapsed in tears and self-hatred for behaving like such a whore, or she pulled herself together, forgave her own stupid actions, and showed him just how strong she could be.

There wasn't really much of a decision to be made. He'd pushed her into that display. He'd deliberately played on her vulnerability, alone in a bedroom with him, frustrated...

Her cheeks flared with hot humiliated colour. All right! she thought furiously. So maybe I am frustrated. But that doesn't mean I don't love Edward—or that Edward doesn't love me! It just means Edward and I want to wait until we're married before we start behaving like wild animals.

Forcing herself to be calm, she dragged on her camisole, walked to the dressing-table, picked up a comb and dragged it through her blonde hair. She rearranged her camisole so that she looked coolly respectable, then steeled herself to face him.

He was waiting in the long white sports car, lounging at the wheel, one arm resting on the open window.

Lucy walked to the car, head held high, and got in, slamming the door and looking at him down her nose, deliberately as arrogant as possible.

Randal's hard mouth crooked into a smile. 'A swift recovery. I'm impressed. No self-torture or recriminations, then?'

'None,' she said coldly. 'I didn't instigate that. You did. If anyone deserves to be tortured, it's you.'

He laughed and started the car. 'And what will you tell Edward?'

'Nothing,' she said icily.

'Good,' murmured Randal with a flick of his black lashes. 'That means your relationship with me is already stronger than your relationship with him.'

Lucy glared at him, face colouring furiously. 'It means no such thing! I happen to love Edward and I——'

'Do me a favour,' he drawled, steering the powerful car out through the gates as they swung open for him. 'Stop telling me you love Edward Blair.'

'Why?' she asked, hoping to hurt. 'Does it bother you?'

'Not in the least,' he drawled mockingly. 'I'm only after your body—remember? You can love anyone you want, so long as I get the response I'm after—and it's not romantic.'

Her eyes darted across his strong profile. She felt hurt by that. Although why that should be she couldn't understand, because not only did she not love Randal—she didn't even like him.

'If you're so interested in my body,' she asked in an icy voice, 'why did you stop making love to me just now?'

'I wanted to teach you a lesson,' he said flatly. 'And I believe I did. A lesson you won't ever forget, Miss Winslow.'

'I'll certainly make sure I'm never alone with you again,' she snapped.

'But will you be able to?' he said softly. 'That is the question.'

'Well, if I ever am alone with you again,' she flared, stung, 'I'll just lie back and think of Edward when you start to pester me with your disgusting attentions!'

He laughed mockingly. 'You're the one who couldn't keep her hands off me, Lucy!'

She snapped, trying to hit out at him blindly. 'You bastard! You——'

He slammed on the brakes on the quiet country road and turned to her, catching her wrists and holding them bitingly until she stopped struggling, and gave a gasp of furious pain as she stared with blazing green eyes into his hateful face.

'I'll always win, Lucy,' he drawled mockingly, controlling her with ease. 'But I like to see you fight. It amuses me to see you wriggle so passionately. You look like a furious cat, hissing and spitting.'

'You ought to have been a torturer!' she spat. 'You'd have loved your work!'

He laughed softly, eyes narrowing on her flushed face. 'Am I torturing you, Lucy?'

Her mouth shook. 'I hate you more than any man I've ever met!'

A hard smile curved his mouth. 'That's fine with me. Just don't make me crash the car or you'll never get the chance to stick a hatchet in my head.'

Lucy refused to laugh, jerking her face away, tensely coiled with anger. Randal released her wrists, took off the handbrake, and the car slid away again while Lucy stared furiously out of the window, wishing there was some way to beat him.

They drove back to London in that same tense silence. When they arrived at her house, she tried to get out of the car without saying a word, imagining he would stop her, pull her back for a kiss.

But he didn't. She stepped out on to the pavement, slammed the door, and then just stood there, pale with shock as she watched the white sports car slide away in the darkness.

Why had he let her go like that? Was it possible that he did not intend to come back again? The thought sent a shard of fear and pain through her. She felt suddenly lost, a sick feeling in the pit of her stomach.

Then she went into the house and found it empty. She wondered where her father was, where Edward was. Thinking of Edward made guilt flood through her in waves.

'Oh, God, what have I done...' she whispered, hands flying to her face as the full impact of her blazing, reckless passion with Randal on that bed hit her right between the eyes.

She had betrayed Edward—betrayed their lifelong love, their trust, their betrothal. What kind of girl was she? To behave so wantonly with that cruel, cynical man who had expressly told her he wanted only her body. She despised herself; remembered with horror her desire for him, the feverish way she had pushed his shirt open, buried her face hungrily against his flesh, kissing him, stroking him, lifting her head for another of his blazing kisses, and let him pull her camisole off, touch her bare torso and kiss her breasts.

To prove to Randal and to herself that she was not affected by those moments on the bed, she had compounded her betrayal by behaving as though it meant nothing to her.

But it meant a great deal. She was intolerably confused. How could she behave like that when she loved Edward? If Edward knew... but he must never know. He would be horrified by her wanton response to Randal. And it was clear to her now that she could not fight him. She went up in flames whenever he looked at her—let alone kissed or touched her. It was her body that was the betrayer of her love for Edward—not her heart.

That night, her father came home at midnight.

Lucy heard the taxi drop him, heard the front door close, and got out of bed. Going downstairs in her nightdress, she halted abruptly when she saw his face.

'Daddy?' She stared at him. He was as white as a ghost, with lines of strain at his mouth and eyes. She flew down the stairs towards him with concern. 'Daddy—what on earth is wrong?'

He stared at her as though he had never seen her before. 'Wrong...'

Fear made her dry-mouthed, but she kept her head. 'Come and sit down. You look ill. Can I get you something?'

Gerald Winslow walked slowly, shell-shocked, his movements strangely calm. 'No... nothing...'

The drawing-room was eerily silent as Lucy watched his white, drawn face. She had never seen him like this before. All the spirit had gone out of him. His skin looked cold and clammy. There was no false gaiety, no sophisticated self-mockery, no laughter at all in those pale, frightened blue eyes.

'Something's happened,' she said in a low voice, 'hasn't it?'

Suddenly, Gerald Winslow crumbled. 'I've done a terrible thing!' he whispered, pushing both hands through his blond hair and sinking into an armchair. 'A terrible, terrible thing...'

Her alarm increased. She knelt by him at once. 'What? What have you done?'

His hands shook as he looked through his fingers at her. 'I can't tell you. I promised silence...secrecy.'

'Who to?' she asked, as a shiver of premonition ran down her back.

He looked at her, about to speak, then shook his head. 'I mustn't,' he said thickly, and suddenly got to his feet, looking at her with that white, strained expression. 'Go to bed, Lucy. You'll find out soon enough. For now—you need to rest and sleep.' He moved towards the drinks cabinet, adding roughly, 'God knows, you'll need it.'

Lucy stood up slowly, heart drumming with alarm. 'If this concerns me I have every right to know.'

He clumsily unscrewed a bottle of whisky. 'Darling, please just go to bed.'

'But everything you just said makes it clear that this concerns me!' She was appalled. 'You can't just——'

'Go to bed,' he said in a weary voice.

Anger suddenly shot through her. 'I demand an answer!' she said fiercely, and crossed the room to him, her green eyes blazing.

Gerald looked down at her, his eyes wide. 'You demand an answer...' he repeated slowly, then, 'You remind me of my father. He used to say that all the time.'

He laughed, pouring a glass of whisky. 'I demand an answer, Gerald!' He raised the glass to his lips. 'Immediately, Gerald!'

'Don't laugh at me!' Lucy caught his arm angrily, and whisky spilled on his suit.

There was a brief, appalled silence while they looked at each other. Lucy was watching him, her green eyes shocked and angry, and he was watching her, white-faced.

'I'm sorry,' Lucy said abruptly. Reaching a hand to his face, she touched him gently and said, 'How soon will I find out? When will I be told what's happened?'

'Tomorrow,' he said thickly.

Lucy nodded, then stood on tiptoe and kissed him. 'Goodnight, Father.' She turned and left the room, a peculiar sense of calm coming over her as she went up to her bedroom.

Slings and arrows of outrageous fortune were obviously on their way to her. All she could do was sit back, let them do their worst, and see what she came out of it with.

Whatever was coming—she would cope with it.

Next day, she felt like someone living in the eye of a storm. Her work at the kindergarten was peculiarly calm. She was waiting for a nuclear explosion, accepting it would come, preparing herself to survive it.

When she got home, she saw Randal's long white sports car outside her house, and her heart nose-dived with a strange mixture of fear and excitement.

He was waiting for her in the drawing-room, standing by the mantelpiece, dark and powerful in a black suit, hands thrust in trouser pockets, a brooding expression on his hard, handsome face.

'Close the door, Lucy,' he drawled coolly when he saw her.

'Where's my father?' she asked flatly.

'He's out. And we're alone. Now close the door and come in. I have something to tell you.'

She closed it, lifted her head, waiting for the blow.

'Your father is bankrupt,' he said flatly, going straight for the jugular.

Lucy went white, her legs weak beneath her. 'How do you know about it? You're just——'

'Because he banks with me.' The blue eyes were penetrating.

'Banks with you!' Lucy gasped, appalled. 'I don't believe it! His bank is Chartered Mallory and——' She broke off, only realising the connection as the words left her lips. Of course. Why had she never put the two together? Mallory...

'Not only is he bankrupt,' Randal said coolly, seeing the dawning of awareness in her eyes, 'but he's now in debt. He began signing markers at my casino a couple of days ago. My staff didn't tell me until last night because they assumed he was a safe bet. But of course, I knew perfectly well he was on the edge of ruin. As soon as I found out, I stopped him, called him into my office, and let him know in no uncertain terms that the party was over.'

'How much does he owe you?' she asked carefully.

'Twenty thousand pounds.'

The curt, blunt statement took her breath away, her face reflecting disbelief. 'Twenty thousand...!'

'It's a great deal of money.' Randal's black brows arched. 'And he must repay it.'

'But he can't,' she said tautly. 'You know perfectly well he can't. He has no income, no——'

'He has this house,' Randal said bluntly.

She whitened further. 'No! This house must never be sold. It was my grandfather's. He left it to us; I grew up here, so did my father! It's all we have left and——'

'Sentiment,' he said tersely. 'I deal in cold hard cash. So does the rest of the world. If he doesn't repay me, I'll take him to bankruptcy court.'

Fury shot through her. 'You would, too, wouldn't you! You'd do that! Humiliate him, destroy what little self-respect he has left and——'

'It's his self-respect,' he said cuttingly. 'He's responsible for its welfare.'

'But you know very well that he couldn't help himself! And now he can't pay back that money because he hasn't an income. He's not qualified to do anything—he's never had a job in his life!'

'That's not my problem,' he drawled. 'I just want my money back.'

Lucy struggled to retain self-control. Moistening her lips, she said thickly, 'Isn't there some other way? I realise it's a great deal of money, but can't it be repaid in instalments? I'd be willing to give you half my wages every week and——'

'That's hardly a feasible solution,' he drawled sardonically. 'The weekly wages of a nursery-maid wouldn't keep me in shirt-buttons.' His hard smile was cruelly mocking. 'Although I appreciate the gesture.'

Hatred welled in her veins, but she struggled to control it, racking her brains for some other way out. She couldn't just stand by and let her father be destroyed. Certainly not publicly. London society had long since learned to despise Gerald Winslow. All the friends they had counted on while her grandfather was alive had deserted them long ago. The horror of bankruptcy court... he would never survive it.

'There is, of course, another way,' Randal drawled lazily. 'Although I doubt very much that you'll agree to it.'

She looked at him and a quiver of fear went through her. 'Well?'

His face was suddenly expressionless. 'You could marry me.'

For a second she thought she had misunderstood. She turned the words over and over in her mind, trying to put them together in a different way so they would mean something else.

'As we're neither of us in love with each other,' he said sardonically, 'I don't intend to propose properly. I think we both know why I'd be marrying you.'

'Sex?' she choked out bitterly.

'Of course,' he drawled softly, eyes mocking.

Her mouth shook. 'But why marriage! Why not just demand that I—that I——' She couldn't finish, her face colouring scarlet.

Randal laughed at her softly. 'Because at first, I thought you were an exciting little conquest to amuse myself with. I expected the attraction to pall. But after your performance yesterday, I can see you're exactly what I've been looking for in a wife.'

Her voice shook. 'You're saying you want to marry me because——'

'You're a lady in public,' he said softly, 'but a whore in the bedroom.'

She sucked in her breath. Suddenly, she was walking across to him, eyes blazing, her hand slapping him across the face stingingly, and as his head jerked back her heart was crashing with turbulent emotion.

He caught her wrists, blue eyes mocking as he drawled, 'What a little spitfire you are! Don't you like hearing the truth?' He laughed, his black hair falling over his hard forehead as he fought with her. 'That's what you are, Lucy. You proved that yesterday. I could have had you, couldn't I? You wouldn't have put up much of a struggle.'

'Liar!' she choked out bitterly, fighting. 'I won't listen——'

'You practically tore my clothes off!' he taunted.

'You made me do it!' she blustered, face burning with rage and humiliation. 'You made me do it!'

'You can take a horse to water,' he drawled softly, 'Or should I say—a whore.'

Somehow she got her wrist free and slapped him again, harder.

His teeth met and he jerked her hard against him. 'Don't you hit me again, you little bitch, or I'll prove what I'm saying by taking you up to bed immediately and giving you what you so obviously, desperately *want*!'

Lucy was almost blind with hatred. But his words terrified her, and she controlled herself, not hitting him again though she longed to. For a long moment they stood in hectic silence. Lucy was breathing hard, her heart hammering violently, her hands shaking on his broad shoulders.

He looked down at her, a hard smile on his ruthless mouth. 'Good girl! Now what's your answer? Will you marry me and be my whore, or shall I let your father go down the drain?'

Shaking, she asked bitterly, 'Don't I even get time to think about it?'

'No,' he said implacably. 'You answer now and stick with whatever you decide. If you refuse me—I'll drop you, your father and the whole Winslow family straight down the plughole.'

'I'm in love with Edward, you ruthless swine!' she said in thickly choked despair. 'Doesn't that mean anything to you?'

'You were in love with him yesterday, and it didn't stop you rolling around on the bed with me,' he drawled jeeringly.

Her eyes closed in abject self-hatred and fury. Bending her head, she breathed hard, weighing up her options. There were none, though. Even she could see that. If she didn't marry Randal, her father would be ruined, and might even die of humiliation. He wouldn't find employment. He'd just sit in this house getting more and more depressed, poverty closing in on him, selling off furniture bit by bit until in the end he'd have to sell the house. His life would wind down like a clockwork toy until, in the end, there would be nothing left. No money, no self-respect, no dignity... nothing.

'Well?' Randal was watching her. 'What's your answer? Yes or no?'

Bitterly, she looked at him. 'Yes, damn you! You know I have no choice. Of course I'll marry you! What else can I do?'

Slowly, his hard, cynical mouth moved in a smile of mocking self-satisfaction.

'What will you tell Edward?' he drawled, laughing softly.

Hurt shot through her. 'Don't laugh at me, you swine! Isn't it enough that I've agreed to marry you?'

'No,' he said, eyes gleaming with mockery. 'I told you I would relish my victory when it came.'

She shuddered, staring at him hotly through her lashes as that betraying pulse began to beat at her throat and wrists. How could a man so cruel excite her like this?

'And now it's time to put my brand on you,' Randal drawled. 'I've arranged an appointment to choose your ring. Shall we go?'

She was shocked. 'You were very sure I'd say yes!'

'Oh, very sure,' he laughed. 'I'm saving your family from ruin, after all!'

'Only temporarily,' she said, eyes bitter. 'My father still has no money and has to live. Even though I'm agreeing to marry you—what will he do? He's never worked, he can't get a job, and——'

'You just leave that to me,' Randal drawled sardonically. 'I have a little plan in mind for your father.'

Lucy studied him warily. 'You have?'

His brows arched. 'I want that money back. Twenty thousand isn't chicken-feed. Besides—it's time your father learnt money doesn't grow on trees. I'll get him a job and make him pay back every penny.'

'But he's not qualified for anything! He's——'

'Capable of working,' he cut in flatly. 'It's just a question of putting your father in the right job and letting him get on with it.' He glanced at his watch. 'But right now it's time we bought you an engagement ring. Come on.'

They drove to a famous French jeweller's in Bond Street. Lucy was still awash with dark emotion: hating Randal, fearing him, loathing him, excited beyond endurance by him...

Randal selected an oval-shaped emerald and slid it on her finger.

'It matches the flash and fire of your eyes,' he observed coolly.

'Surely an opal would be more suitable?' she said in a low whisper, hating him and hating his ring, cold and heavy on her finger. 'Don't they signify bad luck and unhappiness?'

'Possibly,' he drawled. 'But that's not our future, is it? We started fighting passionately—I intend to make sure we go on doing just that.'

'Good,' she said tightly. 'I'll enjoy scratching you as often as possible!'

'So long as your scratches are left on my back,' he mocked, 'I'll be happy to receive them.'

Hot colour flooded her face. She wrenched the ring from her finger. 'Choose the ring yourself, then,' she said under her breath. 'I don't care what it is.'

Angrily, she stamped out to the car and got in, sitting in bitter silence contemplating her future. She would be his wife, share his bed—maybe even give him children.

A lady in public and a whore in the bedroom . . . her cheeks stung with self-hatred. How could she live with herself? If she had been icy with him yesterday, if she had fought him off—would he still have insisted on this marriage?

And what was she going to tell Edward . . . ?

CHAPTER SIX

HER father was waiting anxiously in the kitchen when Lucy got home. Randal had dropped her at the door, saying he had work to do at the casino and would be in touch. The house felt strangely empty, and she went into the kitchen believing herself to be alone.

She jumped when she saw her father. 'Oh . . . !'

Their eyes met and held for a long moment. It seemed that illusions were falling from her eyes at an hourly rate. For the first time, she truly felt she was confronting her father as an adult, not a child.

'Is——' her father was nervous, edgy '—is everything all right?'

Lucy studied him for a moment, then held up her left hand. The oval emerald flashed in the early evening sunlight. Her father stared at the ring fixedly, and she saw relief in his face as he looked back at her.

'Are congratulations in order?' he asked with a nervous smile.

Lucy let her hand drop. 'You knew, didn't you? You knew last night.'

He flushed. 'I couldn't tell you.' He raked a hand through his blond hair. 'I gave Marlborough my word.'

Lucy studied him for a moment, then said, 'Would you mind telling me exactly what happened?'

He drew an unsteady breath, turning, walking to the window to look out. 'How much do you already know?'

'Everything where the money is concerned. I know about the twenty thousand pounds you owe Randal. I know you're finally brankrupt——'

'I see.' He smiled, nodding. 'Well—there's not much to tell. Certainly nothing to hide.' He turned, sighing. 'Marlborough summoned me to an interview at his bank yesterday at two. He had a set of print-outs detailing my account and various cheques I shouldn't have issued.'

'You've been bouncing cheques?' She winced.

'I had no idea the money had run out,' he said thickly. 'I knew it was on the cards, but I just shut my eyes and hoped it wouldn't happen. I kept writing cheques, gambling, living the way I've always lived——'

'But you had so many warnings,' Lucy said in quiet despair.

'I didn't want to hear them,' he replied helplessly. 'That's why I signed those markers. I really didn't know the money was gone.'

Lucy gave a deep sigh. Sinking on to a pine chair, she said, 'Go on.'

'Marlborough was icy with me at the bank,' he said, paling at the memory. 'I'd expected it to be a friendly interview after that weekend at Mallory, but of course it wasn't. It was horrifying. He cut me to ribbons, talked about bankruptcy court, made me write down all my assets and added up the total in his head in a split-second.' He gave a weak smile. 'He's frighteningly good at maths.'

'Then what did he say?'

'That I was ruined.' His face was sheened with a film of perspiration. 'That I'd wilfully brought it on myself. That I'd shamed my father's memory and destroyed my daughter's future.'

Lucy's eyes closed. Randal had been cruel, then. Even though what he had said had been the truth, he had spared her father nothing. She could just hear the hard, ruthless voice he would have used.

'I was just struggling to accept that I was facing total penury and social humiliation when he mentioned you.' He was watching her as she raised her blonde head. He cleared his throat. 'He—he said he was prepared to make a deal.'

'A deal...' she repeated tightly, face white.

He flushed. 'He said he might fancy marrying you, and that if he did, he wouldn't take me to court. He said I was to say nothing to you. It was to be your decision. I was to stay out of the picture. He would break the news to you, and I was to go to the casino at exactly seven, and wait in his office.'

'That was last night?' she guessed, feeling sick inside.

'Yes. He arrived at eight. He said he'd reached his decision. He would marry you and I'd be able to pay the twenty thousand pounds back in instalments. Then he told me to write a twenty-page account of exactly how I'd spent my inheritance. Two pages for every year.' He reddened angrily. 'I felt like a schoolboy!'

'That's why you were at the casino until midnight?' she asked.

'Yes.' He gave a deep sigh. 'It's funny, though. Even though I resented writing out that account—it made me look at it all clearly. I felt stronger. And the funniest thing was that I felt almost relieved.'

'Relieved?'

'Yes... as though the madness was over. I sat in that streamlined office on my own, writing out that report, and I kept looking at Marlborough's empty chair, and feeling safe.' He frowned. 'Does that make sense?'

Lucy nodded. 'Someone stronger had taken control.'

He studied her for a moment, then shrugged. 'Well, anyway... he read through my account at ten. He said it was too frivolous. He was very terse with me and slammed out of the office telling me to write it out again. This time I made it more concise and businesslike. He seemed satisfied by it, and told me he would think about my case and come up with a way I could repay him the money.'

'My marriage?' she asked hoarsely.

'I don't know, Lucy.' He looked miserable. 'It didn't seem that way. I think he's prepared to hold back on bankruptcy proceedings if he marries you. But I think he still wants the money back.'

Lucy remembered what he had said and nodded. 'You're right. I think he's going to find you a job.'

He went white. 'A job? A job...?' He ran a dry tongue over his lips. 'But I wouldn't know how. What as? I mean——'

'You don't have much choice now, Father,' she pointed out gently. 'You have to do as he says.'

He gave a deep sigh. Then his eyes searched hers. 'And you? You don't exactly seem like a rapturous bride. Are—are you happy to be marrying him?'

Lucy gave a wry smile, blinking back sudden hot tears. 'I'll have to be, won't I? It seems we neither of us have any choice.'

He looked sick. 'Darling, I feel so guilty! How can you ever forgive me for what I've done!'

'I've always known this would happen,' she said, compassion in her eyes. 'The only unexpected part of it is Randal Marlborough. I suppose in a way I feel relieved too.' Looking down at the emerald on her finger she said hoarsely, 'Although how I'll survive marriage to him...'

'You don't love him?'

'I hate him!'

He winced, put a hand on her arm. 'Darling, he can't be that bad. He's a very rich and powerful man. The women at the casino seem to purr every time he walks past. Don't you find him at all attractive?'

She flushed deeply and said, 'I'm in love with Edward! I always thought I would marry him!'

'Of course,' her father said, shamefacedly. 'Poor Edward...I feel badly about him, too. He's been such a support for both of us. A tower of strength.' He studied her anxiously. 'He'll be distraught when he hears.'

'You haven't told him, then?' she said quickly.

He shook his head. 'Gave my word to Marlborough.'

Lucy got to her feet, wincing, turning her back so he would not see the despair in her eyes. 'I'll tell Edward, then. I'll tell him in person. He deserves at least that.'

Edward arrived at eight, cheerful and hungry, and Lucy was waiting for him in the kitchen. The dinner was timed for eight-thirty, and was bubbling away on the stove.

'Hello, darling!' Edward said, coming into the kitchen. 'What's up with your father? He seems awfully subdued.' He leant towards the oven. 'Mmm! That smells delicious!'

Lucy watched him, white and unmoving.

He did a double take. There was a little silence. 'Lucy? Are you all——?' His eyes fell to her left hand and he broke off, the colour draining from his face. 'What the hell is that?' His eyes shot back to meet hers. 'Whose ring are you——?'

'Randal Marlborough's,' she said blankly. 'He's asked me to marry him.'

His eyes widened. 'What!'

She took a deep breath, lifting her head. 'It's finally happened, Edward. The crash...' She quickly outlined the details to him.

'Oh, my God...!' Edward stared at her, breathing hard. 'I knew it was coming, but I didn't expect debt as well.'

'My father didn't tell you, then?'

He shook his blond head. 'Not a word.'

Suddenly, she frowned. 'But surely you knew how close the crash was? You check all his expenditures daily. You must have known we only had days left before——'

'Of course I knew!' Edward said quickly. 'But I couldn't bear to burden you with it, Lucy.'

'But it affected me!' she said incredulously. 'If it was a burden to hear about—how do you think it feels to have to live with it!'

He raked a hand through his hair. 'Darling, you're so sweet and gentle. Not strong enough to cope. I feel so guilty. You're so highly strung, so nervous, unable to take pressure and——'

She gave a bitter laugh, shaking her head. 'Edward, I always believed you when you said that I was like that. But lately I've been forced to realise that I was only like that because I never had to deal with reality. Now that I am...' Her green eyes slid to his face with regret as she said quietly, 'I find I'm able to. I find I'm quite strong. I find I'm... a survivor.'

His lashes flickered. 'You're going to marry Marlborough, then?'

'I have to,' she said, and gave a pained shrug, adding, 'It's the only way to survive.'

He gave a deep sigh, then took her in his arms. 'Darling, is there no other way?'

'You know there isn't,' she whispered against his neck, her eyes closed as she breathed in the scent of him, aching inside, wishing it were him she was marrying, not Randal.

He held her very close, kissing her. 'I've spent my life dreaming of marrying you. I was a fool to leave it so late. I should have realised another man would step in and take you.'

'I kept trying to warn you,' she whispered, tears pricking her eyes. 'Oh, Edward, if only we could turn back the clock...'

He raised his head and stared down at her, then gave a groan and kissed her, his mouth meeting hers with all the gentle, loving warmth she had grown up feeling so familiar with. Her arms curled around his neck. She wanted to cry, to rail against fate, to pour out her love for him.

Suddenly, he dragged his mouth from hers, and put her from him firmly. 'It's no good!' he said hoarsely. 'We must both be brave. You have to sacrifice yourself, and I have to help you do it.'

Tears slid over her lashes. 'Edward, I can't bear it...!'

'We must make a clean break,' he said raggedly. 'We must just end it, now, before it becomes too painful.'

'No!' She caught at his shoulders as he tried to leave. 'Don't just leave like this! You've been a part of my life forever. How can I just stop loving you and——?'

'Don't tell me you love me!' he groaned hoarsely, breaking away from her and groping blindly for the door. 'Just go into your new life, my darling! Marry Marlborough, save your family, and forget me...' He wrenched open the door, whispering, 'Forget me, my darling.'

The door slammed behind him. Lucy stood there in agony, then ran after him, tears spilling over her lashes.

'Edward!' She caught him at the door. 'Don't go... please...'

He stared down at her, standing in the open doorway, his eyes hellish. 'My God, don't make this harder than it is already. I'm trying to be strong for both of us. Goodbye, Lucy.' His mouth shook. 'I love you.'

The front door slammed and she put her shaking hands to her face as the tears streamed over her white cheeks. His words spun in her mind and she held on to them for dear life. We must be brave... we must be strong...

Her father came slowly into the hall, his face ashen. 'Was that Edward? Going?'

'Yes,' she whispered. 'He says we must make a clean break of it... and I think he's right.'

'Oh, God.' Her father paled visibly, slumping against the wall. 'I'm responsible for all this. All this misery and destruction...'

Lucy drew a ragged breath. 'Don't expect this misery and destruction to last, Father. Randal is already thinking of a job for you.'

He stiffened, shooting her a quick, uncertain look.

She met his stare levelly. 'I expect you'll be working before the wedding itself.' There was a brief silence. Then Lucy said quietly, 'I'll finish the dinner,' and moved past him into the kitchen.

It helped to perform mundane tasks. They ate in silence, both lost in their own thoughts. Their lives were changing so rapidly that it felt as though they were on a roller-coaster. And Edward had been axed from their world as brutally as though he were an unwanted tree.

She winced inside, hating Randal for his selfishness, his cruelty, his ruthlessness. Edward had been so noble and strong. If only she could have married him. If only he hadn't wanted to wait until the crash came...she wondered why he had. She frowned, and then found herself wondering why Edward had not said or done anything to warn her that the crash was literally days away. Then she felt guilty for such disloyal thoughts when he had been so noble. With a sigh, she dismissed them. She might never even see him again, and that hurt so much that she cried silently at the dinner table, her face white as she mourned the loss of her oldest friend...

Randal picked her up the following evening at six to drive down to Mallory Hall. He was stylishly dressed, his suit grey-blue, a dark silk tie knotted at his throat, his jacket open as he walked up the path and rang the bell.

Lucy answered it, her face hostile. 'I'm ready to leave.'

'Well, I'm not,' he said flatly, stepping past her arrogantly. 'I want a word with your father. Where is he?'

Lucy closed the door after him, green eyes hating him. 'Haven't you humiliated him enough? Can't you just——?'

'Did I hear you say you wanted to see me?' Gerald Winslow's nervous voice came from behind them.

Randal lifted his dark head, his face hardening. 'Yes. We'll talk in the drawing-room.'

Lucy said at once, 'I wish to be present.'

'Why not?' Randal lifted black brows. 'So long as you don't interrupt.'

Lucy glared at him but did not reply, instead allowing him to lead her at his usual dynamic pace into the drawing-room, which he dominated, as he always dominated every room he stood in.

He pushed Lucy into an armchair, indicated with a long hand that her father was to sit, too, then strode coolly to the mantelpiece to stand there, hands thrust in trouser pockets, like the head of the family, an arrogant tilt to his dark head. That jagged scar on his cheek only enhanced his air of dangerous power.

'I've found you a job,' Randal said flatly. 'You're to start tomorrow morning at nine sharp.'

Lucy tensed, shooting a quick glance at her father's ashen face.

'May I ask what kind of job it is?' Gerald cleared his throat.

'Social secretary,' he said coolly.

Lucy stared, round-eyed, holding her breath.

'You'll be working for Mr and Mrs Stewart Saxon,' Randal went on at a brisk pace. 'They're a very wealthy couple, racehorse owners, live in a vast manor just outside Newmarket. They hold a lot of charity functions—coffee mornings, cocktail parties, balls. Fund-raising events that need skilful organisation. They also have a vast circle of friends and business acquaintances to entertain.'

Gerald Winslow was sitting forward, eyes bright with excitement, holding his breath.

Randal looked at him coolly. 'Apart from organising and supervising these social events, you'll be required to entertain guests and clients. They need someone debonair, witty, entertaining and well-spoken. I thought you fitted the bill, recommended you, and they're prepared to take you on three months' trial.'

'Well, I...' Her father was flushed. 'I don't know what to say.'

'Try yes,' Randal said coolly, raising an eyebrow.

'Well, yes, of course!' He got to his feet, smiling. 'I'd absolutely love the job. It's perfect for me. Good heavens—I never expected anything like this, Marlborough. I don't know how to thank you.'

Randal gave a hard smile. 'Just get through the three months' trial, make it a permanent job, and stop drinking.'

'Of course.' Gerald nodded at once.

'You *can* stop drinking, can't you?' Randal clipped out.

'Easily,' her father said in a quiet, level voice. 'It was always just an indulgence—never an illness.'

'Good.' Randal gave a curt nod, took a white envelope from his inside jacket pocket and handed it to him. 'Here are the details of the job. Be there at nine sharp. Oh, and Winslow——' He arched wry brows at him, drawling, 'Remember to use the servants' entrance.'

Gerald Winslow blinked, but extended a hand, saying gravely, 'I don't know how to thank you. I shan't let you down.'

Randal shook his hand firmly, his face hard. Then he flicked his blue eyes to Lucy, who was watching in amazement, staring at him and at her father with dazed eyes.

'Ready?'

She got to her feet at once, kissed her father, and left with Randal. The cream silk dress she wore was a plain shift, worn with a matching jacket of the same length and simplicity.

As they drove down to Mallory, she said carefully, 'That's the perfect job for my father. I don't know how to thank you, Randal.'

'I want my money,' he drawled cynically. 'I won't get it unless he has a job that he can actually hold down.'

Her eyes were bitter, suddenly. 'I might have known it wasn't an act of kindness!'

He laughed, eyes ruthlessly mocking. 'Never expect kindness from me, Lucy. You'll only get hurt.'

'You couldn't hurt me if you tried,' she said contemptuously. 'I feel nothing for you but loathing.'

'And desire,' he drawled, sliding one strong hand over her slim thigh. 'But that's fine with me. You may as well know. I only have three priorities in life. One—my own satisfaction. Two—money. Three—sexual pleasure. This marriage will bring me all three now.'

She hated him suddenly more than she ever had before, and pushed his hand from her thigh, heart thudding at the sight of it, so strong and networked with black hairs.

'I must admit I regret you don't come with a dowry or land or a title.' The blue eyes flicked over her slender body with insolent sexual appraisal. 'But you're such a lady in public, and as for the bedroom...' He let the words hang between them, not completing the sentence, his eyes wicked as he laughed softly at the rush of angry colour to her cheeks.

'If you ever say that to me again——' she began in a voice thickly choked with rage.

'Let me guess,' he drawled. 'You'll slap my face.'

She glared at him and he laughed.

'Save it for our wedding night, Lucy. Plenty of time for passionate expression of hatred then.'

They drove the rest of the way in tense silence. Lucy stared out of the window, consumed with hatred. And to think she had almost admired and respected him for finding such a wonderful job for her father!

Mallory Hall was as ravishing as she remembered it. The red sunset behind its cool white walls made her catch her breath. Her eyes traced the pure lines of the stone and glass, the lined lawns surrounding it, the elegant trees silhouetted against the sky.

Randal's home... his true home. He might not bear the name Mallory, she thought with bitterness, but he bore the hallmarks of that powerful family. The smuggler and the highwayman were part of his character, as they were part of Mallory's with its secret passages and wickedly glamorous history.

'My dear.' Edwina Marlborough was waiting for them in the drawing-room. 'I'm so pleased.' She pressed her scented cheek against Lucy's in a kiss, murmuring, 'I knew it was you.'

Lucy looked at her with a frown of enquiry.

Edwina smiled with those vivid green eyes. 'This is my husband—James Marlborough.'

The austere silver-haired gentleman stepped forwards. 'Edwina was right about you. You're perfect for Randal. It's typical of him to see you, want you and get you.'

'Oh, absolutely!' Edwina laughed. 'Randal always gets what he wants. Even if he has to fight dirty for it. He always gets it in the end.'

'Did he win you by fair means or foul?' James drawled, laughing too. 'On second thoughts—don't answer that! I'm sure the phrase "all's fair in love and war" is one Randal wouldn't hesitate to quote in that rakish way of his. He really is a true Mallory.'

'Kindly stop talking about me as though I'm not here,' Randal said flatly, striding to the drinks cabinet. 'And where the hell are the servants? This decanter is empty.'

Edwina turned to him with a smile. 'Don't be autocratic, darling. Just because we all know you're a swine, there's no need to go around pretending to be Bluebeard.'

'I don't think he's pretending at all,' Lucy said tartly before she could stop herself, and glared at Randal.

James laughed, blue eyes dancing. 'Well, well, well! So your love affair has been quite a battlefield.' He leant forwards and kissed Lucy's cheek. 'Welcome to this family of ambitious misfits, my dear. We none of us truly belong here. None except Randal, of course.'

Edwina said, 'And now Lucy is about to join us. What are your plans, my dear? Will you take a leaf out of Lady Eve Mallory's book and help your husband in his ruthless pursuit of money and power?'

'Who was Lady Eve?' Lucy asked, frowning.

'Her portrait hangs on the stairs,' Edwina told her. 'The blonde beauty with rather wicked green eyes. She was married to Lord Anthony—the Highwayman.'

'They had a very interesting love-life,' Randal drawled, a hard smile curving his mouth. 'Lady Eve used to pretend to be his doxy.'

'Doxy?' Lucy frowned, mystified.

'It's another word for mistress,' Randal said softly, eyes mocking her.

Hot colour flooded her cheeks.

'Randal, such language!' Edwina sighed, shaking her red head.

'Sorry, Mama,' Randal drawled. 'I was teasing my innocent fiancée. I find her blushes irresistible. They make me want to say wicked things to her.'

Lucy's blush increased to scarlet.

Edwina smiled at her, then deftly said, 'When exactly is the wedding, Randal? You said you'd selected a date——'

'August the first,' he said coolly, handing Lucy her drink, a small martini, his fingers brushing hers and making her jump visibly.

'August the first!' Lucy said, taken aback. It was only three weeks away!

'You remember, darling,' Randal murmured. 'I'm sure I told you.'

She just stared at him. He knew perfectly well that they had never discussed a date.

'As Lucy's mother is no longer alive, I thought you might like to help her with the wedding arrangements, Mama,' Randal told his mother coolly.

Edwina looked at her. 'Would you like my help, Lucy? Please don't be afraid to say no. I don't wish to interfere in——'

'I'd welcome your help, to be honest,' Lucy said with a faint, wry smile. 'I've never organised a wedding before, and have no idea where to start.'

'How marvellous!' Edwina said, smiling. 'In that case, I'd be delighted to help. Where would you like to hold the wedding? In London? Or here? Or is there somewhere else?'

Lucy hesitated. She thought of London, of her home and her life there, and all she could feel was darkness; the memories of slowly drowning and being unable to save herself still too vivid in her mind.

'I think I'd like to hold it here,' she said slowly, frowning, amazed to hear herself voice it.

'Good,' Randal said softly, watching her through those carved eyelids. 'I'd hoped you'd say that.'

Her green eyes darted to his face. Her heart skipped a beat. She watched him through her lashes, her eyes intense, and wondered what life would truly be like as his wife.

Later, as they drove back to London, she thought of the speed with which all this was happening and shivered. Her life was almost unrecognisable, and every change seemed to trace inexorably back to Randal, and their first meeting at the casino.

'So how did Edward take the news?' Randal drawled with a barbed smile as the car sped towards the lights of London.

Lucy looked at him, startled. 'Edward...' She realised she had almost forgotten him tonight while in Randal's mesmerising company.

'I take it you told him,' he said mockingly. 'Was there a passionate kiss accompanied by tears and vicious comments about me?'

'What do you expect?' she asked, deliberately trying to get at him, her eyes dark. 'I'm in love with Edward. He's in love with me. You've effectively torn us apart.'

His hands tightened on the steering wheel, but he smiled lazily. 'So long as there are no more passionate kisses and tearful scenes. You're mine now, remember. I won't have you seeing him, Lucy. At least not until the wedding reception.'

'I doubt I shall ever see him again,' she flung accusingly. 'He was so hurt he couldn't bring himself to stay once he knew I was marrying you.'

'My heart bleeds for him!' he drawled in a barbed voice.

'He was strong and very noble about the whole thing!' she said hoarsely. 'And you have no right to laugh at him! He certainly behaved with more decency than you ever have!'

His eyes narrowed. 'Strong and noble? What do you mean?'

She looked away at night-lit London, the orange street lamps flashing past as they left the motorway and drove on to the wide four-lane road that led to the city.

'He said we had to make a clean break,' she told him resentfully. 'That it would be easier that way for both of us.'

'Do you mean he's disappeared?' Randal asked slowly. 'For good?'

Her eyes threw hatred at him. 'I'm sure you're delighted!'

He frowned, narrowed eyes on the road as he drove in silence, and Lucy looked away from him, her mouth trembling. She hated him for laughing at Edward like that. After what he'd done—didn't he have any sense of guilt?

If only Edward had married me, she thought again, aching inside. Why didn't he? Why did he insist on waiting until the crash came...?'

A frown touched her brow and she felt those questions pushing at her again. Why had Edward waited? Why had he not warned her that the crash was just around the corner? And why had he maintained for so long that she was nervous, highly strung, unable to cope with reality...?

Uncomfortable feelings rose up in her, fluttering at her like black butterflies, and she pushed them away, pushed them down, refusing to look at them.

Edward had been her friend—Randal was her enemy.

It was as simple as that...wasn't it?

CHAPTER SEVEN

LUCY didn't see Randal alone again for the next three weeks. He was always on the periphery of life, it seemed. Taking her to Newmarket to see a race, driving her down to Mallory at weekends to see Edwina, dropping by at the Saxons' to check on her father... but never alone with her. Not once in three weeks did he kiss her, touch her, pay her any romantic attention.

Of course, she began to hunger for his kiss. Frequently, she would catch herself staring through her lashes fixedly, staring at his mouth, longing to feel it against hers again. It began to drive her mad. Did he want her still? The wedding was going ahead; all the invitations had been sent out, the caterers hired, the dress was in preparation—yet Randal had totally distanced himself from her.

In an effort to forget her confusing feelings towards Randal, Lucy buried herself in the wedding arrangements. She handed in her notice at the kindergarten, and was relieved when they found a replacement almost immediately. She also became very friendly with Edwina.

'Of course, Randal was always ambitious,' Edwina sighed one night. 'But even I had no idea he would become this wealthy, this influential.'

'Are you pleased, though?' Lucy asked with a frown. They were lounging in the drawing-room of Mallory at midnight, surrounded by wedding paraphernalia, the floor strewn with sketches and lists.

'Very pleased,' Edwina said softly. 'Especially as he's marrying you. He's thirty-three now. Time he formed a family, settled down, had children. After all—what's the point of all his ambition and hard work if he has no one to leave it to at the end?'

Lucy's green eyes clouded. 'He does work awfully hard...'

'Much too hard,' Edwina agreed.

'I've barely seen him since we got engaged,' Lucy confessed, frowning, angrily aware that it sounded as though she missed Randal, which of course was nonsense. She hated him.

'My dear, don't worry that he's been too busy to see much of you lately. He's just trying to get everything out of the way in time for the honeymoon.'

Lucy thought of the honeymoon, and felt her heart skip massive beats at the thought of him making love to her. She hated herself for wanting him, but could not fight the gradual injection of him into her bloodstream. Like a drug, he was now becoming necessary to her. And his absence only made her need stronger.

The wedding day dawned bright and sunny. Lucy had stayed overnight at Mallory in the west wing. Edwina arrived to help her dress. She felt like a sacrifice.

Her blonde hair was pinned up in a cascade of silvery curls, pearl and diamond earrings glittering at her lobes, a pearl and diamond tiara holding the long antique lace veil in place.

'You look lovely,' Edwina said, a tear in her eye.

The dress was a fitted satin off the shoulder gown. Tiny white satin rosebuds lined the décollatage, the cut of the dress accentuating her slender hourglass curves, the long train sweeping behind her as she walked down the stairs of the west wing and stepped into the white limousine with her father, who looked splendid in a grey morning suit and top hat.

'You've made me proud,' Gerald Winslow said, clutching her hand as they drove to the church. 'And so very happy. Without you, none of this would be possible. My job, my son-in-law, my financial salvation...' His pale eyes searched hers anxiously. 'Darling—you will be happy with Randal, won't you?'

Pain shone in her green eyes. 'I'll be very happy.' What else could she say? He wasn't strong enough to hear the truth. And what good would it do to tell him?

Sunlight streamed across the altar through stained glass saints, the scent of orange blossom permeating the village church. Lucy walked up the aisle on her father's arm, trembling with nerves.

Randal turned as the music swelled. He looked magnificent in a grey morning suit, his dark hair haloed by the sun, his blue eyes penetratingly intense. As she reached the altar, her father stepped aside with a proud smile, handing her to the man who was to replace him as the strongest male love in her life. The tragedy was the way he looked down at her, his face hard and somehow austere, only the blaze of the blue eyes betraying any emotion whatever. He did not love her, nor she him.

As they turned to the altar, the sun streamed through the blood of a martyr, casting a warm red glow on Lucy's face. The music stopped, a hush descended on the church, and the priest began to speak, his voice deep and calm as it echoed among the stone walls and arches. Lucy repeated her vows, not glancing at Randal, and when he spoke his voice sent shivers through her.

He was turning to her, taking her left hand, the cold metal of a platinum ring gliding on to her finger, and her eyes shot to his, brilliant green with passionate awareness of her helplessness against him.

He met that gaze with powerful intensity, and his hands lifted the veil, his dark head bending as though in slow motion until that hard mouth closed over hers in a brief, searing kiss.

'I've won,' he said under his breath, and the glitter of mocking triumph in his eyes made her blood stir.

Bells rang out. They were walking down the aisle, man and wife. People clustered around them as they stood on the green in brilliant hot sunlight. Photographs were taken. Ducks and swans glided across the pond on the village green opposite the church. Cars glittered expensively along the lane.

They drove to Mallory for the reception, in a white limousine decked with silk ribbons. Randal studied her with a certain feudal pride in his new possession.

'You look so lovely,' he said softly, blue eyes moving over her. 'I don't think I've ever wanted to undress you more than I do at this moment.'

Anger and excitement flared in her eyes. He had barely been near her for three weeks...she wanted badly to be kissed by him and knew it showed in her face...

'Slowly,' he said, leaning towards her, a hand under her chin. 'Very slowly...and with infinite care. You excite me unbearably. Mistress Lucy...my little doxy...' He laughed softly, his mouth close to hers. 'I could make love to you until doomsday!'

'Oh, yes?' she asked thickly, eyes flashing. 'Then why haven't you wanted to kiss me for three weeks?'

There was an abrupt silence. Hot colour flooded her face as she realised what she'd said. Then she saw Randal's slow, mocking, triumphant smile.

'And you're angry about that, aren't you?' he mocked, his mouth close to hers. 'You want me to kiss you...don't you?'

Lucy shivered, her lips parting in unconscious invitation.

'Ask for a kiss,' he taunted her, mouth brushing hers tormentingly. 'Or you won't get one.'

'Go to hell!' she choked out, heart pounding with desire.

'Remember last time we kissed?' he said under his breath. 'On the bed at Newmarket?'

She breathed faster, eyes dilating.

'How frustrated you were then,' he mocked, his mouth tantalising her deliberately, kissing her lightly, moving away, never unleashing the full force of his passion. 'How you writhed and twisted and tore at my shirt. And I haven't touched you since then, have I? Not once.' His mouth tormented her, his hand stroking her naked throat as the blood pulsed round her body. 'How frustrated are you now, Lucy? How much do you want me to make love to you? How much...?'

'I hate you!' she whispered hoarsely, mouth shaking. 'Kiss me!'

He stared for a moment, passion blazing in his eyes, then he bent his head and kissed her hungrily, a rough gasp in his throat as his hands pulled her slender curved body against him in the luxurious rear of the car.

Her hands were in his dark hair; she was gasping with desire, her mouth moving hungrily against his, oblivious to everything but his kiss, her heart pounding as they slid together.

'Missed me?' he asked thickly against her passionate mouth.

'No!' she denied hotly, fingers threading through his black hair. 'I was glad to be rid of you...glad...'

His mouth closed hungrily over hers again and she moaned, sliding back against the seat as he obliterated her, his strong hands moving over her body in the satin dress, making her heart pound violently as she welcomed him with reckless, blazing, intolerable passion.

Suddenly, he raised his head, darkly flushed.

Slowly, it dawned on Lucy that the car had been stationary outside Mallory for some time. The chauffeur was sitting in discreet silence. The butler was standing outside the car, waiting expressionlessly.

'We'd better go in,' Randal drawled thickly, 'or they may start without us.'

Lucy was silent with shock as he moved away from her, straightening his tie, running a hand through his hair. How could she have been so passionately involved with that kiss? She hadn't even noticed the car stop.

Randal motioned with a cool hand for the car door to be opened, and it was. They went inside. Other guests arrived. The ballroom filled up, people taking their places at the long series of beautifully laid tables while champagne was served with the wedding breakfast.

Gerald Winslow's speech was brilliantly received, his head held high as he held his audience captivated, and Lucy watched him with a prick of tears in her eyes.

The tables were moved aside. Randal whirled her away to dance. The touch of his hard body against hers was like fire as she moved in his arms, tense, silent, pulses beating.

'I notice a distinct lack of accountants at this wedding,' Randal drawled in her ear as they danced.

Her eyes shot to his accusingly. 'I sent him an invitation but he didn't reply. After the way he was treated, I don't blame him.'

'You wouldn't blame him if he stuck a knife in your ribs,' he said flatly, eyes hardening. 'According to you, Edward Blair can do no wrong.'

'That's unfair! He stepped aside very gracefully when you forced me into this marriage.'

'A little too gracefully for my liking,' Randal said flatly. 'And I'm not impressed by his continuing grace. If I'd been in his position, I would have at least put up a fight to keep you, if not actually punched my rival in the face. But he didn't do anything. Not a damned thing.'

'Edward genuinely loved me,' she said fiercely, hands curling on his broad shoulders. 'That's why he went away and stayed away.'

'And I suppose that's why he ignored his wedding invitation?' he sneered. 'Yes, I can quite see that. One always totally ignores the people one genuinely loves.'

Hot colour flooded her face. She wanted to hit him. 'He must be in agony,' she said thickly. 'His life has been destroyed by you. He's lost everything he had—a job, a family and a future.'

'Really?' he drawled unpleasantly. 'That must be why he's spent the last three weeks moving into a luxury apartment on Park Lane, buying a black Lamborghini and being seen out on the town with a sexy redhead every night.'

He broke away from her as the music ended, hard mockery in his eyes as he saw her shocked white face.

'I don't believe you,' she whispered, appalled.

He looked at her for a second, then turned and walked away from her, leaving her stranded on the dance floor, almost swaying under the shock of what he had said.

It couldn't be true... couldn't. The implications were horrific. Like a ghost, she found herself walking to her father. He was the centre of attention, standing among a group of wealthy socialites, talking about his life as social secretary to the Saxons, telling racing anecdotes and dropping names.

'Father...' Her white hand touched his arm, her eyes enormous as she looked into his face. 'I must speak to you.'

'What is it, darling?' Concern shone in his eyes and he at once moved aside to speak privately.

'Have you heard anything from Edward?'

He shook his pale head, frowning. 'Nothing, darling. I thought he'd turn up for this, but of course——'

'Father, what was his financial position?' she asked, dry-mouthed.

'Not good.' Gerald grimaced. 'In fact, that's why I felt so guilty. I helped ruin the boy. He must have suffered very badly from my crash. I wish I could see him to apologise, help, make amends.'

'But surely he earned a good salary for himself?'

'Oh, no,' he said, frowning. 'I was his only client, and I barely paid him enough to live on.'

Lucy whitened, swaying, and her father at once reached for her.

'It's all right,' Randal's cool, strong voice said deeply behind her as a pair of hard hands slid to her waist to steady her. 'I've got her.'

'I think something's wrong,' Gerald said in rapid alarm. 'She's awfully pale...'

'Wedding nerves,' Randal drawled mockingly, turning Lucy in his arms, a gleam of insolence in his eyes. 'I just told her it was time to get ready to leave. Our honeymoon flight leaves in two hours.'

'Is Edwina helping her change?' Gerald asked, looking around for her.

'Yes,' Randal said above Lucy's head. 'Better give her a shout.'

Seconds later, she was whisked upstairs to one of the bedrooms by Edwina Marlborough. The beautiful satin gown was discarded, replaced by the suit she had chosen to go away in: a green silk fitted suit with a peplum that accentuated her slender hourglass figure.

'I'm so glad he chose you.' Edwina gave her an impulsive hug, waves of scent clinging to her soft skin. 'You're everything I dreamed of in a daughter.'

If she knew the truth...but Edwina must never know. Downstairs, her father held her in a strong embrace, obviously moved, and whispered good luck. Then the guests spilled out on to the steps of Mallory as Lucy and Randal ran out to the car in the early evening sunlight.

'Rome is perfect for a honeymoon,' Randal observed as they drove to the airport. 'It's a city that takes my breath away, every time I see it. I'm sure you'll fall in love with it.'

'How nice,' she said in a tense voice, and turned her face from him. The things he had said about Edward were still spinning in her mind like a madness she could not accept. If it were true...but how could it be? And how could she believe Randal anyway? He had a vested interest in casting shadows over her relationship with Edward. He knew she still loved him and he wanted to break that love, shatter it with any weapons he could find. When she returned from this appalling honeymoon, she would find out if Edward really was living that lifestyle. Then, and only then, she would make her decision about whether or not he was—oh, she could hardly bring herself to think it—treacherous.

They landed in Rome. It was eight o'clock Italian time. The sun blazed down over the city. A limousine met them at the airport and whisked them away.

As they drove into the eternal city, Lucy caught her breath, as Randal had said she would. Triumphant music seemed to play in her mind as she saw the gleaming white stone of achingly beautiful buildings, monuments, cathedrals...round every corner...on and on...white steps and towering statues and every time they turned a corner there was another building that stopped her heart, until she was reeling under the impact of such classicism, modernism, antiquity...

The hotel was in the centre of the city. Lucy was tense with excitement and nerves as they were shown to the bridal suite. It soared above the city, a long white suite of impossible luxury, and, as she looked out of the wide windows, she knew she was going to fall in love with Rome.

'We'll unpack after dinner,' Randal said coolly behind her.

Glancing through her lashes, over her shoulder, she saw him lounging against the door, a curious expression on his hard face, and her mouth went dry with abrupt desire.

They ate dinner in the magnificent dining-room, surrounded by musical Italian voices and cool marble. Randal ordered champagne. Lucy could barely taste her food, and left most of it, her heart pounding as she thought of the night ahead.

Afterwards, they went up in the lift, and the tension was intolerable. Randal unlocked the suite door, brooding eyes following her as she walked past him. Her pulses were throbbing hotly at throat and wrists. She heard him close the door and she turned.

They stared at each other in breathless silence.

'Time for bed,' Randal said softly, and her heart stopped beating. He moved towards her with the predatory grace of a lion, absolute power and terrifying justice in his strong, handsome face.

Lucy backed. 'I don't want to——'

'Yes, you do.' His hands reached for her.

'No!' Fear leapt in her green eyes as she evaded him.

'Come on, Lucy,' he drawled in that hard voice. 'It's our wedding night. You knew I'd make love to you. That's the whole point.'

'That's why I don't want to let you do it!' she said heatedly, backing towards the open door of the vast white bedroom as he advanced on her. 'It isn't right! No marriage should be based on sex alone! It should be based on love and respect!'

He laughed mockingly, striding after her. 'As your marriage to Edward Blair would have been? Oh, I can just see it now! Him robbing your father blind while you cook and clean for him like Cinderella!'

'You shut up about Edward!' she blurted out in suddenly fierce emotional confusion, shaking as she backed towards the large white double bed. 'You're trying to insinuate things about him! Terrible things! But I won't listen!'

'No, I know you won't!' he bit out, eyes blazing. 'I sometimes wonder why I bother to tell you that black is black and white is white, because you have a capacity for self-delusion that I find quite staggering!'

Lucy fell on to the bed with a shocked gasp.

Randal knelt on it on one knee, his other long leg staying on the floor as he watched her in the sudden electrifying silence that vibrated between them.

'Well, I think it's time I ripped all the illusions from your eyes,' he said under his breath, and jerked her green silk skirt halfway up her slim thighs.

Excitement pulsed through her. 'You're primitive!' she said thickly.

'So are you!' he drawled. 'And it's time you faced it.' The dark head swooped, his hard mouth closing forcefully over hers.

She fought him, hands hitting his powerful shoulders. He trapped her body beneath his, thrusting one hard thigh over hers, his hand on her waist, his mouth moving commandingly over hers.

'Get off me!' Lucy wriggled in angry excitement beneath him. 'I hate this...hate you...'

He laughed, his mouth burning against hers. 'Really? Then why is your heart beating like a sledgehammer?'

'It's not,' she denied hotly, but her hands curled on his broad shoulders and she was already kissing him back.

'You don't want me to touch you?' he taunted softly, and unbuttoned her jacket, very slowly, kissing her mouth as he did, his tongue slipping between her parted lips as he stroked her breast, slid the lacy bra cup down, took her hard, pulsing nipple between finger and thumb.

'Oh, God...' she moaned thickly, breathing faster, hot needles of excitement throbbing in her.

He smiled mockingly, stroked her breast, his mouth tormenting her with that slow, sensual kiss and she just breathed faster and faster, her heart banging harder and harder, while he taunted her with his expertise.

'Want some more?' he whispered against her mouth.

Lucy moaned, felt his strong hands slide to the zip of her skirt. Madness set in. She was frenzied, feeling him unzip the skirt, then ease it slowly, tormentingly over her hips while she clung to his broad shoulders, breathing thickly, staring at him through her lashes with hot, glazed eyes.

Her half-naked body was pressed slowly against his, his hard thigh parting her slim thighs until the hot pulsing centre of her body was throbbing against him with unbearable need.

'You'll make love to me,' he said thickly, and his strong hands slid down to cup her buttocks.

Lucy gave a long, hoarse cry, and suddenly her hands were in his dark hair. She was kissing him hungrily, her mouth open beneath his. He kissed her commandingly, his hands stroking her erotically.

Sweat pricked on her skin. Drowning in need, she was kissing him greedily, unbuttoning his shirt, pulling it apart and dropping it to the floor, running her hands over that hard-muscled chest and down to the taut stomach below.

Her body seemed to move against his of its own accord. She was fire in his arms, arching as he ran a hard possessive hand down over her naked spine, down to her taut buttocks, and she pressed softly against his hardness, beautiful and wildly out of control, wearing nothing but virginal white lingerie.

'Randal...' She was gasping against his mouth. 'Randal...'

He shed his clothes, sliding naked against her, fondling her buttocks as he pressed her against his body, and she almost sobbed with need, delirious now, moaning as he moved strong hands up to stroke her breasts, then unhook the white bra, slowly remove it while she moaned, eyes closed, feeling her breasts bounce free, the erect nipples grazing his hair-roughened chest.

'Do you want me?' he taunted against her mouth.

'Yes, yes...' she whispered thickly, and moaned out loud as she felt him ease the white silk panties down over her thighs.

Slowly, his naked body slid between her quivering thighs. 'Are you primitive?' he demanded, pushing her slowly on to her back, his hardness sliding against the wet silk of her entrance.

'Oh, yes...' her voice panted in abject surrender. 'Yes...'

'Yes...!' he said thickly, and entered her, making her cry out in pain and pleasure, her nails digging into his naked back as he took her, and she found herself moving in greedy, wanton pleasure against him, naked and abandoned and impaled on his body.

Excitement spiralled. The room fragmented into splintered colours. Her heart was slamming. She was flung headfirst into violent, dark ecstasy, panting hoarsely as her body jerked like a rag doll's against his and every hot, wet spasm left her wallowing in pleasure, her mouth open and her eyes squeezed shut and her hands slipping on his shoulders, and she was lost, utterly lost, writhing against him like the whore he had said she was.

When the storm was over, she came to from a reverie, her body flooded with pleasure, shaking in liquid heat beneath him as he drove for his own satisfaction, his face a hard mask of desire.

Her shaking hands moved over him, encouraging him to experience that ecstasy that had just been hers. She wanted him to feel it...wanted to see him wallowing in pleasure as she had done.

Her mouth kissed the damp throat, her fingers slid down his naked spine; she heard him gasp as she slid them down to his buttocks, dug her nails lightly into him and then he gave a guttural shout and slammed hard against her, his body rigid.

Lucy watched his face, breathless with wonder. In the throes of ecstasy his face was contorted. He was out of control, completely real, completely human.

Emotion flooded her with unexpected force. She moaned his name, watched him give one last hoarse cry. His damp head fell to her shoulder and he dragged air into his lungs, his heart slamming so hard that she thought he might die.

Minutes ticked past in a silence of harsh breathing and pounding hearts.

Her hands cradled his head. She was holding him suddenly in her arms as though she loved him. Emotion was flooding her unstoppably, as though she was falling in love...

Randal raised his head. 'Welcome to the land of the living,' he said deeply. 'Are all your illusions gone?'

She stared at him through sweat-damp lashes. 'Ripped away...'

'Every last one, Lucy?' The hard voice mocked her. 'What about the fair accountant? Do you still believe he was your knight in shining armour?' He laughed thickly. 'His horse limped and he was wall-eyed, but no doubt you believed you could fix that with love.'

Stung, she said bitterly, 'My feelings for Edward are none of your business.'

'Little Miss Fix It!' he drawled with a barbed smile. 'No doubt that's why you hate me so much. You've got nothing to fix.'

'Except your filthy mind,' she said fiercely, wanting to hurt him suddenly, just as he had hurt her with his unbearably clever words.

He laughed mockingly. 'Oh, I'm the only person in this bed with a filthy mind, am I?'

Her face ran with hot colour. 'You made me do all that just now——'

'I made you submit,' he said flatly, 'to your own desires.'

'But I wouldn't have submitted if you hadn't forced me to!'

He gave a shout of laughter, his hair-roughened chest moving as he bent to kiss her, amused. 'Typically illogical. You're intensely feminine, aren't you? Not a shred of logic in that beautiful blonde head.'

Fury made her eyes blaze. 'Don't patronise me, you chauvinist!'

'Realist,' he corrected in a languid drawl, smiling sardonically.

'Realist, then!' she snapped, hating him. 'And I'm only in bed with you because you forced me into this marriage against my wishes. Just as you forced me to—to do all of that against my wishes.'

'But that's the essence of being primitive,' he said softly, his mouth taunting hers with a slow, sensual kiss. 'Thought dissolves...instinct takes over...physical drives override your better judgement...' His blue eyes mocked her ruthlessly. 'And good little girls become bad.'

She trembled beneath him, her pulses picking up the pace as she looked into those penetrating eyes, responding even as her mind fought him, her feelings rising up in a clamour of hatred and desire.

'Is that what happened just now, Lucy?' he whispered against her ear, his tongue snaking out and making her shiver as his hands slowly began to stroke her body. 'Did you lose your mind in a landslide of desire?'

'Yes!' she hissed bitterly, her heart beginning to thud faster.

'And how you fought it!' he mocked. His hand found her breast, fondling it, making her moan in languorous protest. 'You don't know your own body...' he said thickly, kissing her. 'But I'll teach you to understand it. And to understand mine.'

'I don't want to understand any of this!' she whispered, eyes closing, head tilting back even as she spoke.

'Yes, you do,' he said thickly, his body hardening, filling her again as she gasped, tensed, her hands instinctively clutching his tautening buttocks.

'Oh, God...' She found herself kissing him, her heart thudding.

'You don't want to be good, Lucy.' The dark voice stroked her pulses like a silken devil. 'Not with me. Not tonight. I've always appealed to your baser instincts. You want to be bad every time you look at me. Don't you?' His mouth moved against hers as he whispered thickly, 'Don't you...? Say it...'

'Yes, yes...' She was moving as he started to move, desire spiralling, taking her over, her hands clutching him as excitement flared into fire between them and the long night began...a night of exploration, pleasure, and wanton, greedy ecstasy.

CHAPTER EIGHT

IN THE morning, Lucy woke in a haze of sensual warmth. Randal's powerful arms were around her, his body warm against hers, so masculine and strong and hairy. She felt intensely feminine, aware for the first time of the softness of her skin, the beauty of her slender curves and the pleasure of being a woman.

He slept. Lucy looked down slowly at his body against hers. Memories of last night flooded in on her. She could still hear his hoarse cries of pleasure. She remembered how she had been lost in a recurring, endless grip of hot excitement, losing control again and again, her body completely in his hands.

She remembered at one point that she was drowning again in dark ecstasy, and she had thought dazedly, How much more pleasure... how much more...? But still it had not ceased. Minutes later, she had been aroused again by giving him pleasure, encouraging him, exciting him, wanting him to feel as she felt, until the whole night became a ceaseless exchange of pleasure.

How well she knew his body now. She shivered with excitement as she lay there, staring down at him, remembering how she had learnt to touch him in certain ways, wanting to hear his rough gasps, hoarsely whispered words of desire, and finally the guttural cries that made her hair stand on end with excitement as he went over the brink into ecstasy, clutching her to him with hard hands that shook.

'Good morning,' his deep voice drawled, and she gasped, eyes shooting up to his face to meet those piercingly blue eyes and feel the hot rush of colour to her face.

'Oh! I thought you were asleep!'

'I was,' he agreed, and drew her against him for a kiss, his lips warm and firm on hers. 'Don't worry. I woke an hour ago and admired you at my leisure. Why shouldn't you do the same?'

Her colour deepened and she said huskily, 'What time is it?'

'Midday,' he said with a glance at his watch. 'We made love until just before dawn, then collapsed, not surprisingly.' The blue eyes teased her. 'You were quite incredibly exciting. I shall call you Venus.'

'Don't...' she protested, eyes flickering shut with embarrassment.

He laughed, one hand sliding over the white satin curve of her hip. 'You have no right to blush after last night, Venus.'

'Stop it!' she whispered, pulses leaping already. 'Last night was different... I was helpless... it was dark...'

He laughed again, sliding her over on to her back. 'And now it's daylight, so you feel inhibited,' he said softly against her ear, his body very hard against hers and arousing excitement as he slid against her. 'I must break a new inhibition, and I must do it at once... kiss me...'

Lucy moaned in excited protest, and as her mouth met his she gave up all pretence of wanting him to stop, her body clamouring for more pleasure, unbearably involved with him now, hurtling on a roller-coaster of feeling as she clung to his broad shoulders and made love with abandon, crying out his name as he took her to that intoxicating, addictive ecstasy.

Later, they got up, showering together, their bodies more real now than skin had ever seemed to her as he washed her sensually and she washed him, enthralled by every inch of him, staring at his chest in fascination as she watched the warm water wash the soap away.

'How many muscles are there in your chest?' she asked curiously.

'I don't know offhand,' he drawled lazily, his eyes on her face.

She trembled under his gaze unaccountably and looked away, feeling very shy, swamped with powerful feelings which she neither understood nor wanted to understand.

They dressed together. He was ready first, wearing an impeccably cut lightweight grey-blue suit, his white shirt open at the throat. Lucy was dressed in a light blue silk shift dress, seated at the dressing-table applying light make-up.

Randal lay on the bed in silence, watching her, a faint smile on his hard mouth. She was acutely aware of him. What was happening? Why did she feel so close to him?

They had a late lunch. They were both starving and ate hungrily—rich sauces over beautifully cooked veal, washed down with full-bodied red wine. Afterwards, they sat in fulfilled silence, looking out at the sun-drenched city.

'What do you want to see first?' Randal drawled lazily.

'It's your favourite city,' she said with a shrug, trying to prove an indifference she did not feel. 'You decide.'

He took her to St Peter's. The taxi dropped them in fierce sunlight at the edge of the cobbled circle. Lucy was breathless with awe, walking with Randal towards the vast towering cathedral, surrounded by gleaming white stone, statues of saints etched against a piercingly blue sky.

'This is the most beautiful place I've ever seen,' Lucy murmured, staring up at the white statue of Christ.

'See the Vatican guards?' Randal indicated the men in fifteenth-century blue and yellow uniform at the white gates to that fabled city.

'I wish we could sneak in,' she admitted, laughing. 'I'd be utterly fascinated.'

He laughed. 'You'd be utterly thrown out on your ear, too. Nobody gets in there.'

They toured the hushed marble beauty of St Peter's. Randal pointed out Michelangelo's *Pietà*. It took over an hour, and they emerged into the brilliant sunshine, going straight to the Vatican museum round the corner, eventually shuffling with hundreds of others into the Sistine Chapel to stare at that famous ceiling.

'Let's go to a *gelateria*,' Randal drawled as they walked along hot Italian roads surrounded by crumbling beige buildings. He found a very beautiful and very expensive café on a curving main street. They sat down outside at a gaily coloured table with a parasol to shield them from the sun. Italian voices lilted like music all around them.

'*Si, signore*?' asked a smouldering Latin beauty.

Randal gave her an encompassing glance of amused appraisal. '*Due gelati di cioccolato e nociola, per favore*.'

Lucy glared at the girl as she pouted at Randal. When she had gone, she said, 'I didn't know you could speak Italian.'

'It's a very sexy language,' he drawled, eyes mocking her. 'Of course I speak it. I'm attracted to anything sexy.'

'I noticed,' she said, arching blonde brows. 'That waitress was practically bursting out of her dress.'

He shot her a teasing glance. 'You sound almost jealous.'

'Just trying to be realistic,' she said resentfully, averting her green-eyed gaze. 'After all—it's the only reason you married me.'

'And how well you lived up to it last night,' he drawled softly.

Hot colour flooded her face. 'I'm just performing my wifely duties,' she said tightly.

His smile grew barbed. 'Anything rather than admit you enjoyed it.'

Her flush deepened.

'Randal!' a throaty female voice purred next to them. '*Come stai, mio caro*!'

Lucy's head whipped round to stare as another smouldering brunette in another tight dress bent her dark head to kiss Randal's hard cheek with ripe red lips. A vague sense of familiarity pricked at her mind.

'Apollonia!' Randal said, kissing her as he stood up. '*Va'bene, cara—e tu*?'

Jealousy twisted like a knife. Recognition flashed like shock over her body as she sat there, going first hot then cold as she remembered the girl as the brunette who had danced with Randal at the Mallory Ball.

'This is my wife, Lucy,' Randal was drawling, eyes moving over the tight red dress the girl was spilling out of. 'You met her at Mallory, I believe. A shame you couldn't get to the wedding.'

'*Mi dispiace*,' drawled Apollonia insincerely, glowering at Lucy. 'I was too busy. Too much work.'

'Apollonia is a model,' Randal informed her with a sardonic smile.

'And a very good close friend,' purred Apollonia, flashing him a sultry look. 'But not so good and close if you don't tell me you are here in this city of mine.'

He smiled lazily. 'We only arrived last night. I was going to call you after a couple of days, *cara*.'

Lucy stiffened, going pale as she felt jealousy revolve like a knife. He was going to call her? This sensual, exotic creature who had quite obviously either been his mistress in the past or fully intended to become his mistress in the future. Whatever the nature of their relationship, Lucy could see Apollonia desired Randal, and that he desired her, too.

'But now you see me by surprise, *caro*.' Apollonia twirled one of the buttons of Randal's shirt, pouting up at him. 'And tonight I have a party. You come—yes?'

'Would you like to go, Lucy?' Randal drawled, flicking a sardonic glance at her.

'Why not? We've got nothing better to do,' Lucy said with an indifferent shrug, desperate not to show the fierce jealousy she felt.

'Eight o'clock,' Apollonia said triumphantly. 'My apartment on the Via Veneto.' She smiled and kissed him full on the mouth with those ripe red lips, her sensual body curving as her hands clung to his broad shoulders. '*Ciao*!' Another kiss. '*Arrivederci*!' Another kiss. 'I see you later, gorgeous!' she purred, moving away with a meaningful flick of those sultry black eyes.

Lucy was so jealous that she was almost gibbering with rage. Her eyes looked daggers at the sexy brunette as she swayed away in her tight red dress, and Randal—damn him to hell—watched her with blatant appreciation, a sardonic smile on his cynical mouth.

Suddenly, his gaze flicked back to Lucy. His eyes gleamed. 'You look furious,' he drawled mockingly.

Hot colour washed up her face and neck. 'Well, I think she was rather insolent. All those kisses! She doesn't know our marriage is built on mutual dislike.'

He laughed unpleasantly, sat down again, his eyes probing hers. 'You think she went a little too far, do you?'

'I most certainly do,' Lucy said coldly.

'That's the Italians for you,' he drawled mockingly. 'They're a hot-blooded race. Passionate, sensual, abandoned... you could learn a lot from them, Lucy.' His smile was barbed. 'You look a little frigid at the moment. Loosen up. She only kissed me.'

Her mouth tightened. 'I don't care that she kissed you, Randal. I just think she's ill-mannered and rather vulgar.'

'Then why did you accept her invitation to this party?'

'Because I can't stand the thought of another night like last night,' she said scathingly. 'Why else?'

His teeth met. He was violently angry suddenly. She saw it blaze from his eyes, saw the dark colour invade his face. 'Really?' he bit out thickly. 'Maybe I should make love to Apollonia instead. How would you like that?'

Lucy went white. Pain lacerated her. Her mind screamed the word 'no'. Abruptly, she jerked her head away, breathing hoarsely. I don't care, she told herself, I don't care... I don't care...

'If that's what you'd prefer,' she managed to say icily, 'by all means go ahead.'

A muscle jerked in his cheek. He said nothing, and they continued their tour of Rome with an air of tension that grew to a frazzled edge as they arrived back at their hotel at six.

She thought he might punish her for her continued denials of enjoying his lovemaking. She thought he might throw her across the bed and force her to admit how much she clamoured for him. But he didn't. He coolly went into the bathroom and took a leisurely bath, leaving Lucy to contemplate the party with anger, jealousy and dread.

Had Apollonia been his mistress? Her heart thudded with jealous pain. Of course she had . . . it had been obvious from every curve of her body, her mouth, her kisses. The thought of Randal making love to another woman was suddenly intolerable to her. And there was nowhere to run to escape the influx of emotion she was being deluged under.

They took a taxi to the Via Veneto at eight. Rome was hot and lively, nightlife beginning everywhere. Apollonia's apartment was on the fifth floor of a tall marble building. Voices and laughter floated out from luxurious tall doors.

'Apollonia is something of a celebrity in Italy,' Randal drawled as he rang the doorbell. 'There are bound to be some very famous people here.'

The doors were opened by a manservant in white-gold livery. They were led to a very long high-ceilinged room. The guests were sunflushed and expensive and beautiful. Lucy recognised several faces: an Italian-American director, two actresses and a cluster of models.

'Randal!' Apollonia spotted them, undulated towards them in a tight silver dress that gave her sexuality explosive impact. 'You came!'

'I wouldn't have missed this for the world,' drawled Randal, bending his dark head to kiss her. Apollonia's body pressed against him invitingly. He held her by the waist, his mouth coolly amused. 'You're looking unbelievably gorgeous tonight, *mia cara*.'

'In your honour,' purred the sultry Latin beauty, and cast a dark glance suddenly at Lucy, who was watching in barely controlled rage. 'Oh yes...your wife. We'd better get her a drink, Randal.'

Lucy's blood was boiling like Vesuvius, but she could not show it, must not show it. If Randal guessed that she was this jealous...her pride rose up in furious refusal to let that happen.

'Champagne for you, little wife,' drawled Apollonia, handing her a glass. 'And a friend to talk to.' She drew the famous Italian-American film director closer. 'Michael—this is Lucy. She loves your films.'

'Hi,' Michael Salvatore gave her a firm handshake and smile. 'Are you English or American?'

'English,' Lucy said, aware of Randal watching her, and gave the man a brilliant smile, touching his arm as she said, 'I loved your last film. I saw it three times...'

Apollonia led Randal away. Lucy concentrated on Michael Salvatore, discussing films, Hollywood, finance and temperamental actresses with him. But all the time she was acutely aware of Randal talking closely to Apollonia, smiling at her, kissing her red mouth...

'I've been looking for a replacement all day,' Michael Salvatore was saying later as they grazed on fresh strawberries and the music pounded on and on. 'She just stormed out in a huff and filming is suspended.'

'How annoying for you,' Lucy said, staring in agony as she saw Randal dancing very close with Apollonia. The little witch was clinging to him like a limpet.

'I don't suppose you've ever acted, have you?' Michael was watching her with narrowed eyes.

'Never.'

He surveyed her, then said slowly, 'Come and dance.'

They moved to the centre of the long luxurious room. Michael Salvatore was a handsome man, very tall with jet-black eyes and black hair. He was in his mid-forties now, and a vein showed at his smooth temple, his face made more attractive with lines at those powerful black eyes.

'You look very like her,' Michael was saying as they danced closely, 'and it's not a difficult part.'

She gave a tense laugh. 'I've never acted in my life.'

'But we need an English blonde,' he said frankly, 'and we need her now. Like—yesterday. She's only in four scenes. Trouble is—they're vital.'

Lucy shook her head, smiling and flattered. 'I'm sorry. I'm here on my honeymoon. I can't possibly do it.'

'You're kidding!' he laughed, eyes reflecting shock. 'But where the hell is your husband? Surely he should be glued to your side.'

Lucy stiffened, then said lightly, 'My husband is Randal Marlborough. He's somewhere about.'

At that moment, Randal danced by with Apollonia. Lucy's body tensed with frightening emotions. How could she feel this much . . . how? There was red lipstick on Randal's cheek and his eyes met hers with cynical mockery.

Michael Salvatore did a double-take. He was silent for a moment. Then he said shrewdly, 'Would you like to step on to the balcony for a breath of fresh air?'

Pale, violently jealous, Lucy gave a brief nod. 'Thank you.'

The balcony looked down over night-time Rome, brightly lit, a jamboree of cities—ancient Rome, Catholic Rome and modern Rome, all side by side and gleaming with spiritual power.

'Is that really your husband?' Michael asked suddenly.

She nodded, green eyes flicking to his handsome face. 'And this is your honeymoon?'

She nodded again, a bitter smile on her mouth. 'We got married two days ago!'

Cars drove by, far below. A Lambretta sped to the traffic lights. The road was wide and tree-lined, the night hot and sultry. Michael Salvatore took a card from his top pocket.

'Here's my number,' he said in that Italian-American drawl. 'Give me a call if you change your mind about the part. I need to hear by tomorrow, but I'd certainly give you a test.'

She took it with a smile. 'Thank you.'

He studied her for a moment, then put a hand on her cheek. 'You're very lovely,' he said softly, and bent his dark head to kiss her mouth.

Suddenly, she was wrenched away from him, her eyes flying open in shock to stare at Randal towering over both of them, his face dark red with rage.

'What the hell is going on!' he bit out thickly, bristling with aggression.

'Your wife was lonely, Marlborough,' drawled Michael. 'I was keeping her company. Any objections?'

Randal's eyes flicked over him with contempt. 'Only if you try to put her in one of your appalling films.'

'It goes against my rules,' Michael replied lazily, 'but she's so lovely I think I could break just about every rule in the book for her.'

Randal smiled tightly, took Lucy's wrist. 'Too bad, Salvatore. She's got my ring on her finger, and my brand on her forehead. You keep away from her or I'll punch your handsome face through the back of your cunning little head.'

He dragged Lucy off the balcony, and she struggled angrily. 'Why were you so rude to him? He was kind to me!'

'He offered you a part in his latest picture, did he?' Randal drawled tightly, storming out of the party and slamming the door behind him, dragging her into the lift.

'Yes!' she said angrily as the lift rode down. 'An actress stormed off the set today and——'

'And you look just like her,' he drawled nastily. 'It's not a big part, just three or four scenes, but you could play it and he'd help you.'

She stared at him, struck dumb.

'Yes,' Randal said with a sneer, 'it's a good line and it generally works. But not with my wife.' The lift doors opened and he dragged her out of the building on to the hot, bright Via Veneto.

'Do you mean he does that all the time?' Lucy said faintly, staring at the card Michael had given her.

Randal gave a harsh laugh. 'If you weren't so naïve, I'd be inclined to think you were just plain stupid.' He hailed a taxi, his eyes angry, and bundled her into the back of it, sliding in beside her.

They rode back to their hotel in tense silence. Lucy felt a fool, angry and jealous over his relationship with Apollonia, and even angrier with Michael Salvatore. He had seemed so genuine...

When they got back to the bridal suite, Randal ripped the card from her fingers and tore it into tiny pieces. 'Don't even think about ringing that calculating little bastard!' he said tightly, letting the card flutter in pieces to the floor. 'He'd have you on the casting couch before you knew what had hit you!'

Defiantly, she said, 'Well, why should you care? You spent the whole evening dancing with another woman! I wouldn't be surprised to find you'd made a date with her while we're here!'

'Jealousy!' he drawled, striding arrogantly towards her. 'Your eyes are very green. Any minute now you'll fly at me in a rage.'

'Was she your mistress?' she asked thickly, unable to prevent herself.

'And if she was?' he drawled, sliding strong hands on to her waist. 'How would you feel about that, Lucy?'

'Indifferent,' she whispered, and shivered as his mouth moved over her throat.

'Then why ask?' he murmured tauntingly.

Her hands slid to his strong neck, her face lifting to his. 'I'm your wife, now. I have a right to demand respect from you.'

'And are you going to demand it?' He was mocking, smiling as his mouth brushed hers burningly.

'Yes!' Dry-mouthed, she felt her fingers slide into his black hair, pulling his head down to kiss her properly as she whispered urgently, 'And I won't allow you to have mistresses!'

'Be sure to give me everything I need, then,' he said thickly, eyes blazing. 'Will you do that, Lucy? Give me everything . . . ?'

Her slender body curved wantonly against him. With a thrill of greedy desire she looked hotly at him through her lashes, her mouth parted in blatant invitation.

With a rough gasp, his mouth closed over hers. She opened her lips to receive the hot exploration of his kiss, clinging to him, her body leaping with excitement as she unleashed all those feelings like a tidal wave, exhilarated and knocked off balance by the sheer force of them, moaning under the hot onslaught of his mouth. Randal swept her into his arms and carried her to the bed. When they were both naked, he took her, his body tormenting her with pleasure, her heart in pain as her body rode to ecstasy beneath his.

Later, when pleasure had receded and she lay sprawled against his chest, she thought of Apollonia and felt nothing but pain.

Next day, Randal took her to see ancient Rome. The Forum was virtually intact, semi-ruined buildings strewn with grass and wild flowers, the triumphal arch at the end of the long main street evoking visual images of Caesar, Mark Antony and all the great Roman figures leading processions through the streets.

'I can almost hear them gossiping,' Lucy said lightly. 'Talking about Mark Antony running off with that Egyptian woman...'

'Lovers have been the same since the dawn of time,' Randal drawled. 'Passionate, obsessive, causing scandal and sometimes tragedy.'

The sun was hot on her face. 'Was Apollonia your lover?'

He laughed under his breath. 'Your eyes are going green again,' he drawled mockingly. 'But don't change it. I like to see your jealousy. It's so very exciting.'

Lucy tensed angrily, walking slowly along the ancient Roman streets beside him. 'I'm not jealous, Randal,' she said tightly, smiling.

'You wouldn't mind if I went to bed with her tonight, then?' he drawled with a barbed edge to his voice, his smile hard.

'Of course not,' she said, smiling through waves of acid pain.

'Then why did you make those demands last night?' he drawled sardonically. 'If I remember rightly, you said you wouldn't allow me to have mistresses.'

Jealous pain flared in her. 'I'm your wife now. I have a certain position to maintain. Particularly in the public eye. If you had mistresses, people would find out, and I would be humiliated.'

He halted, his blue eyes hard. 'Nothing personal, then?'

She stopped too, face calm. 'Nothing at all.'

There was a silence. The sun blazed down over them. Lucy studied his tough, tanned face but saw no emotion. That hurt, and she turned from him, moving towards a ruined building with pillars, where grass and wild flowers grew up between the ancient stones that had once been a temple.

'Not that way,' Randal drawled coolly. 'You don't belong in there any more.'

Lucy frowned, turning, a question in her eyes.

'It's the Temple of Vesta,' he mocked softly. 'Virgins only.'

She looked away, eyes blinded by the beauty of Rome and the pain in her heart. How she hated him. And her hatred was growing, changing, becoming unbearable—like an unleashed flood-tide of emotion that she could no longer control.

Struggling to remain in control of her emotions, she focused her attention on Rome. It really was the most marvellous city. It really was pulling her deeper into love with its ancient heart. And there were so many facets of it. Catholic Rome soared in gleaming white stone next door. Modern Rome was there too, fighting for space, with office blocks, cars and technology.

'How can it all still be here?' she said tensely to change the subject. 'Ancient Rome, modern Rome, Catholic Rome...'

'They just didn't knock anything down.' Randal seemed as in need of a change of subject as she, his voice curiously distant.

'All side by side.' Lucy's voice trembled. 'Three cities. Like a multiple personality living side by side in complicated harmony.'

'Yes,' he said darkly, eyes gleaming with some unfathomable emotion. 'Bloody complicated.' He took her wrist. 'Come on. Let's see the Colosseum. It's just at the end of this street.'

As they walked into the stone, honeycombed canyons of the Colosseum, Lucy could almost imagine she heard the faded cheer of the crowds, saw the lions, the Christians and the spilt blood.

Emotions were crashing in on her. No matter how hard she fought, some final, devastating ingredient in the hot sun on the ancient stone and the bloody history of this monument seemed to fuse in her soul to force the truth into her heart like a dagger.

I'm in love with Randal, she thought, swaying with a shocked gasp. I've fallen in love with him.

'Oh, no!' she whispered through pale lips, and felt sweat spring out on her forehead. 'No...!'

Randal steadied her with a frown. 'Are you all right?'

Breathless, appalled, she stared into his strong dark face and the tidal wave of feelings finally broke through, engulfing her in the love she had felt for him all along. It had been dammed up for so long, and she had fought it with every ounce of strength, but now the barriers had broken and it was filling her bloodstream, a rush of love to the heart.

'Lucy?' His voice was sharp. 'Is it the heat? The crowds?'

She just stared at him, speechless, her eyes tracing his features as though seeing him for the first time.

His mouth hardened. 'Let's get out of here. There are too many damned tourists...' He led her forcefully through the crowds, out of the Colosseum and on to the streets. Two policemen on white horses clip-clopped past in blue-grey uniform. Randal darted past them, hailed a taxi and took her back to the hotel.

When they reached their hotel suite, Randal closed the door. 'Lucy, what on earth is wrong?' he asked flatly. 'Something happened back there in the Colosseum. What was it?'

She averted her gaze, flushing.

His hand caught her chin, forced her to face him. 'Tell me,' he commanded.

She looked at him, startled and wary. A reply was necessary. It would have to be a good one. She racked her brains, heart thumping very fast.

'I couldn't help thinking of the Christians thrown to the lions,' she blurted out on a wave of inspiration, 'and comparing it to the way you destroyed poor Edward!'

His face tightened. 'My God,' he bit out, eyes violent-blue. 'Will you never get that little bastard out of your head?'

She gave a hysterical laugh. He had believed her, and she almost wept with relief.

'Don't laugh like that!' he said savagely, his fingers tightening painfully on her chin. 'I told you before we left that Edward Blair had ripped your father off to the tune of at least a million!'

'What...!' she gasped, staring at him, her face white.

'His Park Lane apartment. His Lamborghini.' The blue eyes threw contempt at her. 'What the hell did you think I was trying to tell you? That he'd suddenly inherited a fortune from his long-lost auntie?'

Dry-mouthed with horror, she suddenly saw it was true, but was trapped in her own deception, and had no option but to say, 'I don't believe you! I'll never believe you!' although, of course, she believed every word now.

'Well, that just proves that I married you for your body,' he said bitingly. 'Because there's precious little in your mind to attract me!' His hands shot to her shoulders, dragging her towards him forcefully. 'And now I think I'll just get my money's worth.'

As his hard mouth closed over hers she was already dizzy, a moan of pleasure coming from the back of her throat as he tilted her head back to receive that masterful kiss. Her arms wound around his neck. She was curving against his hard body, her pulses hammering.

Randal lifted her in his arms and carried her to the bed. 'I'll drive him out of you!' he said thickly as he laid her down, arched over her, his powerful body strong against hers. 'By the time this honeymoon is over, you'll have forgotten you ever knew that bastard Blair!'

Lucy submitted eagerly, her head swimming as he pressed her back into the pillows, undressing her as the kiss blazed on and on, and when they were both naked he took her, eliciting cries of ecstasy from her as his hard hands and body wrung torturous pleasure from her.

Later, as she lay gasping against his naked shoulder, she saw Rome glittering in the sunshine beyond her window, and knew she would forever see it as a symbol of her love for this complex, multi-faceted man who was her husband.

Her love for Edward was suddenly laid bare to her. It was a habit—nothing more. Something she had simply accepted from childhood, grown accustomed to, and eventually been blinded by. He had simply always been there, and she had loved him without ever questioning who he really was.

Now that she was in love with Randal, she could stand back and see Edward from an objective viewpoint. Everything Randal said made sense. Of course Edward had been stealing money from her father. Why else would he have delayed his marriage to her? Why else would he have disappeared once the money was gone?

Anger rose up in her. Edward was vile, loathsome, a creep and a liar. She couldn't let him get away with it. She would go to see him when she got back to London, and confront him with this.

But she would never be able to tell Randal.

Her only defence against Randal lay in Edward. He must never guess that she had stopped loving Edward. If he guessed that, he would guess the reason why—himself.

Randal had transformed her into a woman. Edward had tried to keep her as a child. Dependent, obedient, unquestioning, she had given Edward everything and demanded nothing in return.

Randal had freed her...but now she was trapped in a passionate love for him that she could never reveal.

CHAPTER NINE

THE rest of the honeymoon passed in much the same way. Randal took her sightseeing continually, showing her as many facets of Rome as possible. He was an intelligent and amusing guide, reeling off facts in that cool, clever voice and making her laugh with his wicked wit.

She was becoming a creature of the senses, longing for the moments when they were alone together, late at night, and he took her in his arms. He was a drug to her system, and her blood would race at the merest touch, the hint of a kiss.

He made her feel so beautiful, so sensual, so much a woman. Her body clamoured for his touch, she was greedily passionate, craving lovemaking like the whore he had said she was.

By the time they flew back to London, Lucy was a sunflushed beauty with tousled blonde hair, a love-bruised mouth and a penchant for off-the-shoulder clothes.

A limousine met them at the airport and drove them straight to Mallory. She felt a strange sense of alarm, staring out at England's green fields. It was late August, sunny and bright—but this was reality, and she did not know how she would cope with life with a man who did not love her.

Mallory was cool white, framed against a halcyon blue sky, as they drove up the long drive. The grass was very green, red roses grew in vivid colour against the white walls and a gardener was driving around on a red buggy lawn-mower, curving lined patterns on the lawns.

'Darlings!' Edwina was radiant in a purple sun-dress as she greeted them from the drawing-room terrace. 'You're just in time for afternoon tea! Come and join us!'

Randal directed the chauffeur to take their cases up. Then he walked with Lucy across the neat lawn, the scent of fresh-mown grass heady in the hot afternoon.

'My dear, let me look at you!' Edwina said, holding Lucy at arm's length. 'Well, I never! Randal has positively transformed you!'

Lucy flushed deeply, darting a sharp glance at her dark, handsome husband. Was her love becoming obvious? Had Randal himself begun to suspect her new feelings?

'Doesn't she look lovely?' Edwina asked her husband James.

'Ravishing,' James agreed, looming over her with that silver hair and piercing blue eyes. 'And every inch a female Mallory.'

'My dear.' Edwina patted her hand. 'Sit down and tell me all about Rome.'

Lucy latched on to the subject with relief. Animatedly, she talked about the city, trying to make it look as though the combination of Rome and the sun had wrought this apparently obvious change in her. If Randal suspected for one second that it was him, he would guess that she loved him, and the humiliation of that was more than she could bear.

'Did you throw a coin in the Trevi Fountain?' James Marlborough asked with a lazy smile.

'Yes.' Lucy dimpled. 'Randal said you had to throw it backwards, and I couldn't get the hang of it.'

'She ended up throwing a small fortune over her shoulder,' Randal drawled. 'I got a photo of her looking rather het-up about it all.'

'Then I leant on that taxi.' Lucy groaned at the memory.

'And the alarm went off.' Randal laughed. 'Yes, I got a photo of that, too.'

Lucy bit her lip. 'That alarm was ear-splitting and everyone was staring at me. I felt such a fool.'

They sounded like any happy couple returning from their honeymoon. But, of course, the truth was far from that. The only moments of emotion Randal had shown her were when he was making love to her. Apart from when they were in bed together, he had remained the cynical, ruthless and very dangerous man he had been all along—one who did not love her, and had married her only for sex.

'We'll go up and rest now before dinner,' Randal said at five, getting to his feet. 'Will you be eating in, Mama?'

'On your first night home?' Edwina laughed. 'I wouldn't miss it for the world. Welcome home, both of you. This is a new era for Mallory and I couldn't be more delighted.'

Lucy smiled and followed Randal into the house. He led the way, and she was astonished by her feelings for Mallory. Was this vast palatial manor to be her home? It seemed incredible. Suddenly, she felt out of her depth, frowning as Randal strode ahead of her and pushed open the double doors of the master bedroom.

She had seen the master bedroom once, briefly, before they were married. It had alarmed her then, with its stark masculine décor, the dark browns and rich deep reds, the polished oak floor and silk rugs, the tapestries around that magnificent carved four-poster bed and the high, cavernous ceiling with its glittering crystal chandelier.

'You become mistress here tomorrow,' Randal said coolly, watching her. 'My mother will hand over the reins of power in the morning.'

She made a face. 'I don't know how to begin running a house the size of Mallory. I don't even know how many rooms there are.'

'Forty-seven,' he drawled with a slow, curving smile. 'And my mother will help you find your feet. She's been running the place since I bought it a few years ago.'

Lucy studied him, green eyes secretly admiring. 'What do you do with all the other rooms? You hardly need them.'

'I think about them,' he drawled cynically. 'And remember that I was brought up in a two-bedroom flat. It makes me feel good, you see, to get what I want in the end. However long it takes me to get it.'

Her pulses skipped. 'Does that include me, Randal?'

'Of course,' he said softly, mockingly.

She shivered. He was so formidable. Everything had happened just as he wanted it. He possessed her utterly now. She was his wife and mistress in every sense, even though she had initially refused him, just as Mallory had been out of his reach. He had won both by sheer force of ambition and desire. He would always win...

Much later, they dressed and went down to dinner. Edwina and James were waiting for them in the drawing-room.

'Mrs Travers is a gem of a housekeeper,' Edwina confided over dinner.

'I find her rather intimidating,' Lucy confessed with a grimace.

'Oh, she is,' agreed Edwina, laughing. 'That's why she's so marvellous. Whips the rest of the staff into shape, takes no nonsense and follows orders to the letter.'

Lucy's eyes widened. 'You mean all I have to do is give orders?'

'Of course!'

Would she be happy here, though? she wondered. Running a house full of servants, married to a man who did not love her? A sigh broke her lips. If only she could have children...surely that would change things for her?

Later, they went upstairs to the master bedroom, and as Randal closed the door behind him she felt the tension descend between them, his blue eyes following her as she walked across the room.

'Will you be here tomorrow?' she murmured, trying to break the silence, 'to help me find my feet as mistress of Mallory?'

'No,' he drawled sardonically. 'I'll be going to work.'

'London?' she asked at once.

'Newmarket. But I'll drive to London later to check on the casino.'

'So you won't come home till late?' she asked carefully, thinking she might take the opportunity to confront Edward.

There was a tense silence. He was very still, his eyes narrowed on her face.

'I—I just want to know when to expect you home,' she said unconvincingly and lowered her lashes, a flush rising in her cheeks.

He gave her a savage smile. 'You mean you want to pay a visit to Edward Blair at his Park Lane apartment!'

'No, of course not!' she denied hotly, blushing scarlet.

'Not much!' he drawled bitingly, and strode towards her. 'You can't wait, can you? You haven't stopped thinking about him since he walked off with all your father's money and left you!'

'I don't want to talk about Edward with you!' She lifted her chin.

He caught her shoulders in a vicious grip. 'We've only been back in England five minutes, and already we're talking about that——'

'Randal, you're hurting me!' she protested, struggling.

'Good,' he said viciously. 'I want to. It's obviously what you like. Blair's a swine from way back; all he does is hurt you, and you can't keep your stupid mind off him! Well, don't you worry, my darling, I'll be a bastard for you tonight.'

'No, don't...!' she broke out, seeing the dark rage in his eyes.

'I insist!' His hand took the front of her dress and tore it in one violent movement, eyes blazing as he bit out thickly, 'Just for you!'

'Oh, God...' she whispered thickly, swaying, her blood pulsing with intolerable desire as she felt his blue eyes move over her bare breasts and silk briefs where the torn dress laid her bare.

'Oh, yes, I knew you'd love it,' he said thickly against her ear, pulling her struggling body back towards the bed. 'If a bastard is what you want, a bastard is what you'll get tonight.' He threw her on the bed. 'With pleasure!'

Lucy fell on to the bed with a gasp and he ripped the dress from her body, hands moving punishingly over her, making her moan hoarsely, her hands pushing at his broad shoulders as he stripped her naked, his face a primitive mask of hatred and desire.

He didn't undress, just pushed his clothing aside and took her brutally, bruising her soft skin as his hands roved over her breasts and buttocks as he drove into her, and to her everlasting humiliation she reached a wild ecstasy very quickly, gasping out his name as her body writhed in hot spasms against him.

'Oh, God... Randal... Randal.' Her voice was splintering, delirious; she was gasping with pleasure, clinging to him.

'It's all you understand, isn't it?' he bit out hoarsely, slamming cruelly into her, hands bruising her. 'The only way to get through to you...'

She raised her lips, kissing him gaspingly. 'Yes... I want you...'

He gave a guttural shout, jerking against her in agonised pleasure.

When he was spent, he rolled away from her, his face hard.

'Randal...?' She reached for him, wanting to feel that warm intimacy which always drew them together after lovemaking.

'I wanted to hurt you,' Randal said tightly, rearranging his clothing and getting off the bed. 'But it seems I can't do that through lovemaking. You like it too much, don't you, my beautiful little whore?'

Her faced rushed with hot colour. 'Stop calling me that!'

'Why not?' he asked savagely. 'It's what you are. You married me for money and sex, but you love another man—a crook, a cheat and a con-man.' He laughed harshly, his eyes barbaric. 'If I didn't find you so damned exciting, I'd want to put my hands round your amoral little neck and strangle you! I'm certainly beginning to wish I'd never married you, you faithless little——' He broke off suddenly.

There was a stunned silence. His voice had risen in fury until it was hoarse with rage. Now they were left staring at each other, and Lucy was white with pain as she saw the extent of his hatred.

'I don't know how you can fling accusations like that at me,' she whispered bitterly. 'You married me for sex. It was all your idea.'

'Yes, and if I hadn't come along you would have been happy to stay with Blair. Wouldn't you?' His eyes held a savage glitter as he bit out thickly, 'Wouldn't you?'

'He was always there!' she said defensively, angrily.

'And now I'm the one who'll always be there!' he bit out, leaning towards her, his face barbaric. 'Count on it, Lucy. Don't try my patience. I already want to hurt you. It won't take much to push me into wanting to kill you!' He turned on his heel and strode from the room, slamming the door so hard behind him that it rattled in its solid wooden frame.

Lucy lay awake for what seemed like hours. His outburst had appalled her. Did he really hate her so much? Tears burned her eyes, falling uncontrollably. So his hatred would never turn to love, as hers had. That was painfully clear. He wished he had never married her...

It was two a.m. when the bedroom door opened and Randal came back to bed. She lay in the darkness, listening to him moving about, getting undressed, washing in the bathroom, walking to the bed and sliding in beside her.

He turned his back on her and went to sleep. He smelt of whisky.

Pain shot through her. He had stayed up drinking alone, unable to contemplate what he had done in marrying her. The agony she felt was intolerable. When she woke the next morning, Randal was gone.

'He left at seven,' Edwina told her at breakfast. 'In a horrible temper. Snarled at the chauffeur to bring the Rolls, and then changed his mind. Drove off in the white sports car, leaving a cloud of dust.'

Lucy paled, and hid her expression by concentrating on pouring coffee.

'Never mind.' Edwina misinterpreted her anxiety. 'He'll be in a better temper when he gets home tonight. Meanwhile—I've arranged an eleven o'clock meeting with Mrs Travers and the rest of the staff.'

She spent the morning with Edwina, studying household accounts books and the files of each member of staff complete with photographs and personal details. Mallory Hall was run like a business, with the kind of streamlined efficiency she had grown to love in Randal Marlborough.

When she met the staff, she was astonished by how many of them there were. A head gardener, four under-gardeners, six housemaids, a butler, three grooms and of course—The Housekeeper.

Mrs Travers was briskly polite and treated Lucy with great respect, although she never smiled. Various house-maids bobbed and smiled to make up for it, and one of the grooms gave her a distinctly flirtatious look.

'I think I'm going to enjoy being mistress here,' Lucy said when the staff had gone. 'It'll be like a real job, won't it?'

'Oh, good heavens, yes!' Edwina nodded vigorously. 'You have to run a tight ship, Lucy. Randal expects everything to go like clockwork.'

After lunch, the head gardener gave Lucy a tour of the estate. They both sat in his bright red lawn-buggy and drove around the grounds in the hot sunshine. He was a ruddy-faced country man, and he loved his work.

'Well,' said Edwina later that afternoon, 'I think you've completed your work for today. Why not take the rest of the afternoon off?'

Lucy made a face. 'There's nowhere for me to go. I don't have a car and——'

'But Randal left the limousine here,' Edwina shrugged. 'And the chauffeur is somewhere around. Ring him on extension seventeen. Tell him you want to go out.'

Her lashes flickered. She thought of Edward, lying and swindling for years. 'I'd quite like to go to London,' she said casually.

'Very good idea,' Edwina said briskly. 'You do that.'

It was easy to track down Edward Blair. All she had to do was go to his previous address. The elderly landlady had known Lucy for years, and was happy to give her Edward's forwarding address. As she got back into the waiting limousine, she realised it would be dangerous to let the chauffeur know where she was going.

'Park Lane Hilton,' she told him. When he dropped her there she said casually, 'Could you pick me up at seven?'

'Yes, madam.' He tilted his cap respectfully, and drove away.

Breathing a sigh of relief, Lucy took Edward's address from her handbag, and set off to find him.

The apartment building was, as Randal had said, luxurious. A glittering foyer was guarded by a liveried doorman. Luckily, he did not try to prevent her from taking the mirrored lift, and she was able to ride up to the tenth floor without Edward being warned of her arrival.

It was six o'clock as she rang the doorbell of his luxury apartment.

He opened the door, expensively dressed, suntanned, a smile on his face. It died as he saw Lucy.

'Hello, Edward,' she said, coldly polite. 'May I come in?'

His lashes flickered. He stepped back and held the door open for her in silence. Lucy walked past him into a luxurious hallway, then through double doors into a fifty-foot penthouse living-room of such breathtaking luxury that she felt waves of rage swamp her.

Edward closed the doors. 'How did you get my address?'

'Your previous landlady.' Lucy turned, face tight with dislike.

'I should have told her not to reveal it to you,' he said. 'But it never occurred to me that you might try to find me.'

'I wouldn't have done,' she said icily, 'if Randal hadn't told me about your sudden windfall.'

'My windfall...'

'How much did you steal from my father?' Her eyes were contemptuous. 'One million? Two?'

'A gentleman never tells,' he drawled with open mockery.

Lucy's mouth tightened. 'You're very sure of yourself, Edward. What did you do? Burn the account books?'

'As a matter of fact,' he said lightly, 'all the account books were lost in transit when I moved here.'

'What a shame,' she said sarcastically. 'No chance of prosecuting you for grand larceny, then?'

'Careful,' he murmured. 'You'll find yourself in court for slander.'

'And where do you tell the authorities you got all this money?' she asked angrily. 'Pennies from heaven?'

His eyes narrowed. 'Your father would have frittered it all away in the end. What difference does it make if I helped the process along a little?'

'He trusted you!' she spat, green eyes blazing. 'He took you into his home and his family and treated you like a son!'

'Big wow!'

'My God.' Her heart was thumping with fury. 'You really are a nasty piece of work, aren't you? I can't believe I nearly married you. I'd rather have married a weasel.' She walked towards him, her eyes scathing. 'You're a crook and a thief and a con-man, Edward Blair, and I'm ashamed to have known you.'

'You have no right to sneer at me,' he said flatly. 'You married Marlborough for his money and we both know it.'

'I was forced into marrying him,' she said icily. 'It's true—I hated him at first, and resented my marriage. But I've grown to respect and love him since then. He's cynical and arrogant and ruthless—but he's made his money through ambition and hard work.' Her eyes raked him with blazing contempt. 'Not through conning his surrogate father out of millions!'

Edward went scarlet. 'Don't try to justify your marriage like that! I know what really happened! I was there—remember!'

'No, Edward,' she said tightly. 'You were never really there. You were an actor living behind a mask—nothing but a tacky little con-man.'

'I wasn't!' he said furiously. 'I was bloody brilliant!'

'Brilliant?' She laughed contemptuously. 'If you think it's clever to behave like a snake, you're a fool. Snakes have slimy skin and crawl around on their bellies. That just about sums you up, I think.'

His eyes blazed. 'I got away with millions and you can't prove it!'

'I don't need to prove it,' she said icily. 'I know it. My opinion is worth far more to me than seeing you behind bars, and right now, Edward, my opinion of you isn't worth repeating. As for my father's opinion—well, I'm going to see him tonight. I'll break this gently to him. He'll be hurt at first, but it won't take long for him to loathe and despise you, just as I do.'

'But he won't be able to do anything about it,' Edward sneered. 'And neither will you!'

'Oh, I think we can do quite a lot,' she said, arching her brows. 'For instance, we can completely erase your memory from our lives. Get rid of everything that reminds us we ever knew you.'

'I'll be so hurt,' he mocked unpleasantly.

'Yes, you will, Edward,' she said quietly. 'Maybe not now, maybe not for a few years. But eventually——'

'Rubbish!' he snapped, his skin reddening.

'Have you got any other family?' she asked coolly. 'Or is this it? Is this all you've got to show for your life?' She waved a hand to the apartment.

There was a silence.

'We may not be able to prove what you did,' Lucy said quietly. 'We can't take you to a court of law and demand justice. But there's such a thing as natural justice, Edward, and it always works. I don't know how or when you'll get the bill for what you've done. But you will get it. And I have a feeling that bill will be loneliness and regret.'

His colour deepened. He said nothing, his mouth a bitter line. Lucy flicked her lashes from him with icy contempt, then walked coolly towards the door.

As she took the lift down, she felt as though a great weight had been lifted from her shoulders. All those years of loving Edward—purely out of habit and familiarity. Edward had taken advantage of that, and of her father's affection. Now the slate felt wiped clean, leaving her free to step into the future untainted by what Edward had done.

Smiling, she walked out into the sunlit courtyard, and saw the long white sports car waiting for her.

Her heart stopped dead. She went white. Randal was opening the door, getting out, his face hard and expressionless. He stood there, magnificent in his grey business suit, bristling with unleashed anger.

Lucy walked over to him with trepidation. 'What a coincidence, Randal, I——'

'Don't try to pretend you haven't been seeing Blair!' he cut in tightly. 'The chauffeur came straight to the casino and told me where he'd dropped you. As soon as I heard the words "Park Lane" I knew where you'd gone.'

She swallowed, her throat dry as ashes. 'I only arrived here half an hour ago. You can't think——'

'I think you've been doing exactly what I knew you'd do,' he said through his teeth. 'Seeing your little con-man lover!'

'He's not my lover!' she said, whitening. 'He never has been and you know it.'

'Shut up and get in the car,' he said icily.

'I wanted to see my father,' Lucy began. 'I rang him and said I'd be there at six——'

'We'll go to see him together,' Randal bit out, eyes blazing, and Lucy had no option but to walk to the passenger seat.

The car shot away into the glittering London traffic. Randal drove with a face like barbed wire. He was so angry; she could sense under that civilised business exterior the primitive desire to hit her, and her misery was unbearable. He really hated her... regretted marrying her... what future was there for them now?

They went into her father's house a short while later, the anger clinging to Randal like a dark cloak. Her father didn't seem to notice it. He was bright, cheerful, delighted to see them and full of stories about his busy, exciting new life.

'The coffee morning went off without a hitch.' Gerald Winslow looked debonair in his grey suit. 'I greeted all the guests, kept an eye on the staff, helped with the raffle...'

Lucy listened with affection, glad to see him so happy. Randal loomed ominously at the mantelpiece, a look of brooding anger on his face as his eyes moved back and forth between Lucy and her father.

'Heard anything from Edward?' Gerald suddenly asked, and an electric silence fell.

'Ask Lucy,' Randal drawled unpleasantly. 'She's just seen him.'

'Really?' Her father turned, staring. 'But where is he? How is he?'

She hesitated, then said carefully, 'He's not very well, Dad. But I'd rather discuss this with you another time. I promised Edwina I'd be home for dinner at eight-thirty.' Looking at Randal, she added, 'If we leave now, we should just make it.'

'But, Lucy——' her father began, frowning.

'I'll come to see you tomorrow,' Lucy said at once. 'I promise.' She got to her feet, her eyes pleading with Randal. 'Can we go now...?'

They said their goodbyes, then went out to the car. Randal watched her with narrowed eyes as she slid into the passenger seat. They drove down to Mallory in tense silence.

Suddenly, Randal said flatly, 'Why didn't you want to tell your father you'd seen Blair?'

She tensed. 'I will tell him. But I wanted to do it privately.'

His teeth met. 'Without me around to hear the loving details?'

Lucy looked away, her face pale, unable to reply. What could she say? If he knew how she really felt about Edward, he would guess that she had stopped loving him—and started loving Randal.

'You may as well know,' Randal said tightly, 'that I've informed the authorities about Blair. They've already begun investigations.'

She turned, eyes wide with hope. 'What...!'

'Don't look so shocked, my love,' he said savagely. 'Did you really think I'd let the little bastard get away with grand larceny?' He laughed harshly. 'I've no doubt he spun you a believable tale about how he got that money. You believed him because you're too much in love with him to see him for what he really is. But I can assure you the Inland Revenue won't be as gullible. They'll march him off to prison in double-quick time.'

Lucy wanted to fling her arms around him and shower him with kisses. Quickly, she looked out of the window, her pulses leaping, love flooding her, so proud of him that she couldn't speak.

'You're not to see him again,' Randal said in a voice thickly cloaked with rage, as the car shot along the motorway. 'He's on a one-way visit to prison, and I won't have you getting dragged into it. Do you understand me?'

'Yes,' she said quietly, her face averted.

That night, for the first time since their wedding, Randal did not make love to her. Lucy lay in the dark beside him, pain eating at her heart.

Next morning, she woke up to find herself alone in the vast four-poster bed. He not only regrets our marriage, she thought in despair, he's actually beginning to tire of making love to me.

She almost felt like throwing herself out of the window. Was this the way their married life was to be? Distrust, isolation and despair? At least when they had been making love every night, they had had an intimate bond powerful enough to ease the pain.

Now, they had nothing. She refused to give in to the pain, though, and spent the day adjusting to her life as mistress of Mallory.

At six, she left with the chauffeur for London. Her father was waiting eagerly for her to tell him what had happened with Edward. Gently, she told him the truth.

'I can't believe it...' Gerald Winslow was white, severely shocked. 'How could he do it? I loved and trusted him. Treated him as a son...'

'You'd better sit down,' Lucy said, concerned, as she led him to an armchair. 'It's a terrible shock, I know, but it's the truth, Dad. It was Edward all along.'

'I could understand the odd pound or two,' he whispered, 'but two million?'

'There's no real proof about the amount,' Lucy told him quietly, 'but Randal believes it's close to two million.'

'And you say he's alerted the authorities?' he said with a bitter smile. 'Well, I hate to say it, but I'm glad. I hope they nail him to the wall. When I think of what I did for that boy—— '

The doorbell rang.

'I'll get it,' Lucy said, her heart beating with abrupt violence. 'I expect it's Randal.'

'Is he meeting you here?'

'No.' Lucy went to the drawing-room door, and into the hall, saying as she walked, 'But he knows I'm here, and as he's in London too he probably thought I...'

The words died on her lips as she opened the front door and saw Edward. For a second, she simply stared at him. Then her eyes flared with bitterness.

'Well,' she said icily, 'talk of the devil.'

Edward pushed past her, his face a mask of fury. 'What the hell is going on! I've got the Inland Revenue breathing down my neck, demanding my account books and my bank statements for the last twelve months!'

'You've come to the wrong place for sympathy, Edward!' Lucy said tightly, slamming the door behind him and facing him.

'Is that him?' Gerald Winslow strode out into the hall, eyes blazing. 'My God—you've got a nerve, coming here!'

'It was you, wasn't it?' Edward turned on Lucy. 'I remember you said something about the authorities last night! You must have told them it was an emergency! They were on to me first thing this morning!'

'Good,' Lucy said. 'I hope they lock you up and throw away the key.'

'I'll second that!' Gerald snapped, striding towards Edward. 'Rotten to the core—that's what you are. I took you in, treated you as my son, promised my daughter to you! And this is how you repay me!'

'You would have spent it all anyway, you stupid old drunk!' Edward snapped viciously.

Gerald hit him. Edward stumbled backwards, shocked, a hand to his jaw as he fell heavily against Lucy. She broke his fall, her arms instinctively catching him.

The doorbell rang and, as Lucy gasped, her father strode past her and wrenched it open to reveal Randal, whose eyes blazed with dark rage as he saw her holding Edward in her arms.

CHAPTER TEN

EDWARD staggered for his balance, turning in Lucy's arms, clinging to her shoulders as she supported him with loathing. There was a peculiar expression in his eyes and he looked almost feral.

'Get your hands off my wife!' Randal said through his teeth, and shot across the hall to him, dragging him from Lucy and drawing his fist back to deliver a punch that sent Edward spinning across the hall with a sickening crack. He landed on the stairs, dazed, blood on his mouth. Randal strode over to him, picked him up by the lapels and snarled, 'Prison and a punch in the face isn't good enough for you. I ought to break your damned neck for what you've done.'

'It was you,' Edward said, running a hand over his bloodied mouth. 'You told the Inland Revenue.'

'That's right,' Randal said bitingly. 'And I'll come and cheer when they lock you up.' He hustled him to the door, threw him bodily on to the path and towered over him, bristling with violence. 'Now get in your flashy car and drive back to your flashy apartment. It won't be yours for very much longer. Enjoy it while you can.' He slammed the door, then turned on Lucy, his face barbaric. 'I might have known he'd come crawling back here!' he bit out hoarsely. 'And that you'd welcome him with open arms, you little——'

'Randal!' her father broke in, rushing to him. 'I can't thank you enough for all you've done—investigating

Edward, informing the Inland Revenue. Lucy and I are eternally in your debt for all of this.'

Randal stared for a second, his lips white. 'You know?'

'Lucy told me the whole story not half an hour ago,' Gerald said.

Randal was even more shocked, staring at Lucy as the colour drained from his face, and a dark enquiry formed in his steel-blue eyes. She couldn't meet his probing gaze. She felt sick inside, aware that he would put two and two together and come up with love.

'How much did she tell you?' Randal asked very slowly.

'Everything,' Gerald continued. 'How much Edward had stolen, where he lived, the car he drove.'

Randal was staring at her. 'Did she tell you she went to see him yesterday?'

'Oh, yes!' said Gerald. 'And she really tore twenty strips off him, didn't she!'

'She did what?' Randal said thickly, staring at her.

Lucy's face burned. She couldn't look at him. Now he would know she loved him. The pain and humiliation were too great to bear. She wanted to run from his knowledge, hide her face from his intense gaze.

'She told him exactly what I would have done. That he was a crook, a thief and a nasty little con-man,' Gerald went on. 'I only wish I'd been there to see it.'

'So do I,' Randal said under his breath, eyes boring into Lucy.

'Stay for dinner, Randal,' Gerald said suddenly. 'I'd love to discuss this in greater detail with you both.'

'I'd love to,' Randal said curtly, eyes narrowed on Lucy, 'but I'm afraid I've already arranged to dine at home with Lucy. Some other time, perhaps?'

They left in a tense silence a few minutes later. Lucy felt so exposed, so vulnerable. Randal knew now. He knew everything about her real feelings for Edward. She would have to fight very hard to make sure he didn't guess her real feelings for himself.

The sports car shot out of London and on to the motorway. Neither of them spoke. Tension radiated between them in the luxurious interior of the car.

Suddenly, Randal said coolly, 'When did you begin to realise that I was telling the truth about Edward?'

'I don't remember,' she said thickly, not looking at him.

He gave a brief, harsh laugh. 'Come off it. Of course you remember. When was it?'

Pulses leaping with alarm, she said, 'What does it matter? I realised, and acted on it. That's all that's important.'

'I want to know,' he said tightly.

'Well, I can't remember,' she muttered, face flushing hotly.

'Jog your memory,' he said bitingly. 'Was it after we came back from Rome—or before?'

Her flush deepened. She couldn't lie, so she said nothing.

Randal shot her a savage look. 'Must you be so damned uncommunicative! It's a perfectly simple question. Why won't you answer it?'

'Because I don't want to discuss it with you,' she said, tight-lipped.

'I see!' he said tightly, as the car put on speed. 'You don't want to discuss it with me. Is that why you didn't tell me the real purpose of your visit last night?'

'That's right,' she said, not looking at him.

'Even when I made it clear that I'd set the authorities on his tail?' Randal bit out.

'That doesn't make any difference, Randal,' she said flatly. 'You set them on Edward for your own reasons. Don't try to make our reasons the same.'

'I'm trying to find out why you didn't tell me what was really going on in your head!' he snapped, and the car shot off the motorway towards Mallory.

'I didn't think it was anything to do with you,' Lucy said tautly, staring out at the hedgerows as sunlight dappled them.

'What!' His knuckles whitened on the steering-wheel. 'How can it be nothing to do with me?'

'Because it was never anything to do with you,' she said. 'It was always between me, Edward and my father.'

His teeth met. 'My God, you ungrateful little bitch!'

'Ungrateful!' Her eyes shot to his, meeting his gaze for the first time, fury in her eyes. 'Oh, I'm hardly that, Randal! I show my gratitude to you every night in bed! What more could you ask for from a grateful wife!'

His eyes blazed. 'That wasn't what I meant, and you know it!'

'What else could you mean?' she asked bitterly. 'You certainly don't want me to show love in return for your "chivalry"—do you?'

'Certainly not,' he drawled with a hard smile.

She turned away again, stung. 'Then what do you want from me?'

'I'd just like the truth once in a while,' he drawled tightly.

'Then you should be pleased. Because you just got it. My feelings for Edward and my private conversations with him are none of your business.'

They turned into the gates of Mallory, and the evening sun dappled the long white bonnet of the sports car as they drove up towards that elegant white manor house.

'Feelings for him?' Randal said tightly. 'You mean you still have feelings for that little creep?'

'How many times do I have to say the words—none of your business?'

He slammed on the brakes a few feet from the front door. 'That is my business, damn it!' he swore hoarsely, his colour high and his eyes like burning coals. 'I have a right to know what your feelings are towards the man who's been my rival from day one!'

'I thought you didn't care if I loved him!' she flung bitterly, and leapt out of the car before he could stop her.

Running wildly, she startled Mrs Travers in the hall, who spun, staring after her. A second later, Randal's footsteps were echoing in the hallway as he followed her.

'Lucy!' His voice was a whiplash. 'Come down here at once!'

Breathless, she skidded along the corridor to the master bedroom and ran in, slamming the door behind her, fumbling for the key, her heart pounding. The lock clicked into place. Lucy backed, gasping for breath, and waited for him to hammer on the door.

But he didn't. Seconds ticked past. She frowned, perplexed. Then she realised he wasn't going to come and get her at all. He obviously couldn't be bothered.

Suddenly, the bookcase in the wall sprang open. Lucy spun, gasping. Randal stepped out, a dark shadowy wall behind him, and she realised it was the secret passage he had told her about.

'I might have known you'd live up to the Mallory name!' she said, pulses leaping. 'Secrecy and subterfuge and——'

'Given that I've just thrown the full legal book at your con-man lover,' Randal bit out, 'I hardly think that accusation appropriate!'

Her eyes flared bitterly. 'How many times do I have to tell you! Edward was never my lover!'

'But how you wish he had been!' Randal snarled, and slammed the bookcase shut behind him as he advanced on her.

'What difference does it make what I felt for Edward?' she said fiercely. 'You're my husband now—and my lover. You bought me, you paid for me, and you can do what you like with me.'

'I can't, apparently!' he bit out hoarsely, and strode towards her with demonic purpose in his eyes. 'I can't make you tell me what's going on in your head!'

'Get away from me!' She backed away, her eyes fierce green. 'You don't give a damn about my feelings! All you want is to take me to bed when the mood strikes you.' Her voice grew hoarse, tears burning her eyes. 'And you don't even want to do that any more, do you! You're bored with me! Tired of me and——'

'I'm not bored with making love to you, you stupid little bitch!' he swore hoarsely. 'I'm bored with the sound of your damned schoolgirl-love for that swine!' He caught her shoulders. 'I want to know exactly what happened between you and Edward Blair! Tell me, or I'll——'

'You know what happened!' she said, struggling to get away from him. 'You were there today, weren't you?

You heard what Edward said, what my father said. What more do you need to know?'

He was silent for a moment, a muscle jerking in his cheek. Their eyes met and warred. She felt his fingers digging into the soft flesh of her shoulders.

'Do you still love him?' he asked thickly.

Heat flooded her face. She lowered her lashes, afraid to answer for fear of revealing her true love.

'Answer me!' he commanded harshly, shaking her. 'Do you still love Blair?'

Lucy cried out as she was shaken violently. 'Let me go!'

'Not until you answer me!' He shook her harder, making her head snap back and forwards until something inside her could tolerate no more.

'No!' she shouted hoarsely, and the shaking abruptly stopped.

There was a tense silence.

'No!' Lucy whispered bitterly, tears blurring her vision. 'I don't love Edward any more.' Her anger died abruptly when she saw his face tauten, the bones seeming to push out against that brown flesh, and her heart leapt with a violent hope that frightened her as she also saw the blazing passion in his eyes. 'I...' Her voice seemed to have dried up. 'I...don't love Edward any more.'

'When did you stop loving him?' he asked thickly.

'I...can't remember.'

He breathed harshly. 'I'll shake you till your head falls off, so help me, Lucy! Now tell me—when did you stop loving Blair?'

She felt tongue-tied. 'In...' She broke off, moistening her lips. 'In...in Rome.'

He was motionless. 'Be more specific.'

She flushed hotly, lowering her lashes.

One long hand moved to her chin, thrust her head back. 'Tell me!' he commanded. 'I want the exact moment, Lucy.'

Lucy trembled, whispered thickly, 'I don't want to tell you, Randal. Don't make me... please...'

His hand tightened on her chin. His voice grew strangely husky. 'Why don't you want to tell me, Lucy?'

Her colour deepened. She didn't dare look away from the scrutiny of those blue eyes. But she had to fight to keep her own eyes guarded, not letting her love shine through and communicate itself to him.

'Was it at the start of our honeymoon?' he asked under his breath. 'Or the end?'

Her face turned scarlet. 'The start...'

'The start. I see.' His eyes were intense, his voice taut. 'Could you be even more specific? The first day? The second?'

Lucy closed her eyes.

'Answer me, Lucy,' his voice commanded softly.

She swallowed hard, then said, 'It—it was gradual...I didn't realise I'd stopped loving him until the third day. But... but the process had started before then.'

'On our wedding night?' he asked softly. 'Is that when the process began?'

With a cry of humiliation, Lucy broke away from him, her hands to her hot face as tears threatened to spill over her lashes, stumbling blindly away from him.

'Lucy...!' He shot after her, catching her by the shoulders.

'No!' she cried hoarsely, tears spilling over her lashes. 'I won't let you gloat over your triumph! You know now—isn't that enough for you?'

'Know what?' His hand slid to her neck, pulled her against his hard chest, held her close as his voice said deeply into her hair, 'Tell me, Lucy. Tell me...'

'Oh, why don't you say it out loud, you swine?' she whispered against his chest. 'You must know how I really feel! You've won!' She lifted her head, tears spilling over her cheeks. 'You said when we first met that you'd hunt me down, no matter how long it took, and close in for the kill. Well, this is it, isn't it? The metaphorical kill took place long ago, Randal.' Her mouth shook, her voice grew hoarse. 'I fell in love with you on our wedding night and I hate you for it... I hate you...'

'You love me...!' He stared down at her, his eyes blazing with passion. 'Say it again!'

'No, I won't say it again!' she refused fiercely. 'You've got your kill, Randal—isn't there enough blood in your mouth?'

'There'll never be enough heart's blood, Lucy,' he said thickly, 'and I can never hear you say you love me often enough. I've waited too long to hear it. I think I need to hear it all night long... all tomorrow... for the rest of my life...'

'What...?' She stared, incredulous, hope making her dizzy.

'I fell in love with you months ago,' he said under his breath. 'Long before I asked you to marry me.'

Her breath caught. She felt as though she might faint with shock. 'No... I don't believe it...'

'At first I just wanted you,' he said thickly. 'You were so beautiful and ladylike, totally unaware of your unbelievable sex appeal. When I spoke to you, you were polite and well-mannered. But when I kissed you, you turned into a spitting virago, with flashing green eyes and a temper like a wildcat.' He gave an unsteady laugh. 'I kept wanting to provoke you again. To make you turn into that green-eyed cat. I even wanted you to slap me. Anything—just to see that look of blazing passion in your face.'

She was staring at him, her mouth parted in breathless disbelief.

'When I bought you that perfume,' he drawled huskily, 'I knew you'd pour it all away, and I loved the thought of you doing that. I could just picture your face as you did it, furious and full of fire.'

'You said such dreadful things to me...' she whispered, unable to let go of her fear and believe him.

'I told you,' he said softly. 'I wanted to provoke you. I couldn't resist. I spent hours trying to think of the most scandalous things I could say, and then said them. Your reactions were even more exciting than I'd hoped.'

'You said I'd one day be your mistress,' she accused. 'Don't tell me that wasn't what you really wanted.'

'It wasn't all I wanted,' he said, smiling. 'But it was certainly high up on the list. And you went scarlet and stared at me with those blazing eyes, my darling. My blood pressure went through the roof. I went home in an agony of excitement and planned my next little meeting with you.'

'It was all planned?' she asked dazedly. 'Not impulsive?'

'I knew the minute I saw you that you were a virgin,' he said gently, and touched her soft cheek when she blushed and looked away. 'Or rather—I suspected it. You looked as though your head and body hadn't quite got together yet. I knew it would take a long time to get you into bed with me, and I wanted you so much I knew I was prepared to work like crazy until I got you.'

'Go on...' she whispered, heart pounding as she clung to him. 'I'm beginning to believe you.'

He held her tighter. 'I was bowled over the first time I saw you. I've never felt such a powerful attraction and excitement. I kept staring at you that night at the casino and imagining myself kissing you, undressing you, making love to you... my God, how I controlled myself I'll never know. I think it was because I could see you didn't have the faintest idea what was going on in my mind.'

'I began to suspect,' she said slowly, beginning to believe him, beginning to dare to hope it might be true. 'When you sat down next to me, staring at me with that curious expression.'

A smile curved the cynical mouth. 'I was wondering how far I'd get before you realised and slapped my face.'

Lucy smiled at him through her lashes. 'That kiss was so fantastic, Randal. I hated you for days because I knew I wanted you to do it again and I hated myself for that.'

'I could tell,' he said softly. 'It was mutual, and your innocence was the only barrier between us. I was drowning in excitement when I kissed you that first time—and then you turned into the wildcat. I was almost completely hooked when you ran out, spitting. The next time I saw you, I was even more excited. By the third time I saw you...' He paused, staring down at her, then drawled wryly, 'I was heavily in love.'

She tensed, eyes wary. 'Randal—are you telling me the truth? I couldn't bear it if this were just another hurtful game...'

'My darling,' he said softly, 'I was obsessed with you by the third time I saw you. I can remember saying all those things to you, about how I'd get you in the end, how I wouldn't stop until I had you, and I suddenly realised as I drove away that I meant them. I meant every damned syllable. I pulled up outside the casino and got out of the car, feeling alarmed by how much I meant what I'd said. Then it hit me, as I was walking up the steps. I was in love with you.'

'I can't believe it...' she whispered, afraid to hope.

'I stopped on the steps for a long time,' he said deeply. 'I saw my name above the door in blue neon, and I thought: Lucy Marlborough. Then I saw us living at Mallory, our children playing on the lawn, and I thought: this is it. She's the one.'

Belief rushed in on her and she felt tears of love blur her vision. 'Darling...'

He kissed her deeply, and the love exchanged in their kiss was more powerfully moving and exciting than any sensation she had experienced in her life.

He broke away from her, his mouth close to hers. 'You'd told me you had a boyfriend, and I should have been put off. But being an arrogant swine, I convinced myself you didn't really care about him. I was certain I could break whatever hold he had on you. It was obvious he hadn't made love to you, or proposed marriage—therefore you were free to leave him when I succeeded in making you fall in love with me.'

Her mouth curved in a breathless smile. 'Such arrogance...'

'I know, I know,' he drawled, laughing wryly. 'And I got my come-uppance when I realised you were the serious one in that partnership. I only had to take one look at Blair to see he was a liar and a cheat. But you were blind to him. I knew he was holding you back from adult life and I hated him for that, because I could see you were different whenever he was around. He was stifling your natural personality—all the things I loved about you. Your vibrancy, your temper, your intelligence and your sexuality.'

'I was used to loving him,' she confessed. 'It was just habit.'

'I realised that, too,' he said soberly, his face paling. 'The fight I was going into was against your childhood illusions, my darling, and that was a tougher adversary than any man. I knew I had to break his magic spell by fair means or foul. I chose foul. Your sensuality was awakened by me. You hated me for it, but you never let me down when I launched a seduction on you. I decided sex was my most powerful weapon, so I aimed it at you ruthlessly. It was that which always provoked you into showing your true nature, and I hit you with it mercilessly, knowing it would eventually make you break out of your chrysalis and show yourself.'

Tears stung her eyes. 'My darling, I owe you so much...'

He kissed her, eyes wickedly amused. 'Oh, I enjoyed myself doing it, darling. I loved making you fly at me in a rage that turned so quickly into frenzied desire.' He laughed softly. 'Especially on the bed at my house in Newmarket! My God, that was exactly what I'd taken you there to provoke and I was reeling with excitement when we left. I knew I was on the right track, then. I knew I was winning the battle.'

'Is that when you decided on marriage?' she asked, eyes wary.

'I'd decided on marriage before that,' he assured her, smiling lazily. 'But your response to my lovemaking that day told me you were definitely ready to fall in love with me, too. I decided to take a gamble, push it all to a confrontation point, and force you into marriage immediately.'

'I'm so glad you did,' she said huskily, touching his strong, scarred face.

'So am I,' he said softly. 'I also believed it would flush Blair out into the open for the skunk he was. If your father had just crashed, Blair would probably have been more careful about revealing his ill-gotten gains. But with you married to a very rich man, and your father securely in a good job—he felt safe.'

Her eyes darkened. 'Is that the only reason you got my father that position?'

'Don't be silly, darling,' he said gently. 'I'm fond of your father. He's been a fool, but largely because he's had such a boring life. Many people without a sense of purpose or a job to do fall by the wayside. The fact that your father fell by spending vast sums of money on nothing is irrelevant. I think he was just bored to death. Now that he's got an exciting job and a new life he's shed twenty years and started to stand up straight.'

'He's so happy,' she agreed, eyes shining. 'I can't thank you enough for finding that job for him. And for revealing Edward's true character to me.'

He studied her frowningly. 'Did you really never suspect him?

She hesitated, then said, 'I began to question him within days of meeting you. I knew your presence in my life was the catalyst. I hated you for making me question Edward. But the more you provoked me into losing my temper, the more I questioned him.'

'You'd trusted him all your life,' he said, touching her cheek. 'If anything, you were taught to trust him.'

'Yes,' she said at once. 'That's it. I was taught to trust him, and I felt guilty every time I started to question that trust. By the time you told me, at the wedding, what Edward was really doing, I was ready to believe you.'

'And did you?' he asked, eyes probing her face.

'Yes, but I couldn't face it then,' she said with a deep sigh. 'It wasn't until you made love to me, and I realised I was in love with you, that I was able to stand back and see Edward for who he really was.'

'And that was on our wedding night?' he said, bending his dark head to kiss her mouth. 'My darling, if only I'd known...'

'It was like the way you fell in love with me,' she confessed huskily. 'I began to realise something powerful was happening after you'd made love to me. But it wasn't until we were at the Colosseum that day that the full impact hit me.'

'I knew it!' he said at once, eyes gleaming. 'I knew something important had happened then!'

She smiled, her face flushing as she murmured, 'I was in too deep by then to lie to myself any longer. I felt struck by lightning that day. Everything turned around and I knew I was deeply in love with you.'

He kissed her mouth lingeringly. 'Just as I stopped on the steps...'

'Just the same,' she whispered, and their mouths met in a long kiss that began with slow, sensual love, then fired into a blazing passion that left them both gasping for breath.

'Oh, God,' he said hoarsely. 'I love you...my darling...'

'Randal!' Her fingers pushed into his black hair, her lips raised hungrily to his. 'I love you...make love to me!'

With a rough sound, he claimed her mouth again and the kiss seemed to go on and on as they clung together, swaying, as though they could not get enough of each other.

Suddenly, he lifted her in his arms and carried her to the bed. His face was darkly flushed as he lowered her to the centre, sliding on top of her, a blaze of need in his eyes.

'Wait!' She put her hands to his broad shoulders, gasping, 'What about Apollonia?'

He stared, dazed, breathing thickly. 'Apollonia...?'

'What did she mean to you, Randal?' she asked hoarsely. 'Was she your mistress? Did you love her?'

He drew a breath. 'Apollonia was never my mistress. We met two years ago when I was on business in Rome. I flirted with her because I had nothing better to do. But I wasn't seriously interested. She was always too obvious to appeal to me.'

Lucy studied him through her lashes. 'Yes, I thought she was rather blatant.'

He laughed, blue eyes gleaming wickedly. 'So you were jealous, after all!'

'Violently,' she said. 'And I still might be if you don't tell me why she was here when you held the Mallory Ball.'

'Someone else brought her,' he assured her, smiling. 'I didn't invite her personally. That was one of the things that turned me off her. You may have noticed in Rome—she did all the chasing.'

'And you prefer to be the hunter?' she murmured teasingly.

'Absolutely,' he said under his breath. 'What man doesn't?'

Her heart sang and she wound her arms around his neck. 'Darling—did you mean what you said about children? That you saw us here at Mallory, surrounded by them?'

'Of course.' He kissed her mouth. 'I don't know if it's occurred to you, my darling, but you may already be pregnant. Would that please you?'

'Oh, yes,' she whispered joyfully, 'and I hope I am. I'd love it if our first child was conceived in Rome.'

'Born at Mallory,' he said thickly, eyes intense. 'My darling, you've made my life complete.'

'And you've made me a woman,' she said passionately.

Randal bent his head with a fierce groan of love, kissing her into oblivion. She opened her mouth to him with wild passion, and the kiss flared to fire.

Randal Marlborough was many things—arrogant, cynical, passionate, sexy, ruthless, strong, clever and loving—but most of all, he was hers. Pride soared in her heart. She could see their future together, unravelling like a rich tapestry, with children on the lawns of Mallory in bright sunlight, her father happy and secure in his work, and Randal's wicked ancestors forming the background to their future. He was a fighter, and she was a survivor.

What a wonderful life I'll have with him, she thought, and then her thoughts were drowned by the power of his kiss...